# ALL OF YOUR MOST PRIVATE PLACES

# ALL OF YOUR MOST PRIVATE PLACES

## MEGHAN LAMB

*There will always be a jar of ash.
There will always be an unfit mind.
There will always be a lonely son.
There will always be a humiliated little girl.*

—*Xiu Xiu*

Copyright © 2019 by Meghan Lamb
All rights reserved.

This book may not be reproduced, in whole or in part, in any form (beyond that copying permitted by Sections 107 and 108 of the U.S. Copyright Law and except by reviewers for the public press), without written permission from the publishers.

Book design by Drew Burk.
Cover design by Richard Siken.

ISBN 978-1-948510-34-9

Spork Press
Tucson, AZ
**SPORKPRESS.COM**

# ALL OF YOUR MOST PRIVATE PLACES

I

# THE HI-POINT

When we move into the apartment, I make note of all the buildings on the block, along the walk that feels like ours.

Four thin homes. Then, the Hi-Point building with its gray slab walls, its gray lawn, and its many tinted rows of mirrored windows.

Nothing along our street is anything worth looking at, but when you look at its reflection, gleaming, through the Hi-Point, everything takes on a warm-gold, just-beginning sort of glow.

Although, the parking lot is filled with split brick, crumbled stone, and shards of glass.

•

Tall weeds grow through the cracks.

Some grow as tall as me.

Some, taller.

They grow on and up and they grow into their reflections.

They sway back and forth like pale, pleasant winds, a kind of gentle bobbing bound in movements from some world that I cannot see.

They bob their heads, like stems sprung, springs of movements made of ether, made of shine, some wave that seems to rise up from the glass.

A sense of nothingness waves to me through their warm gold-lit reflections.

Hello, says the nothing.

Hello, hello, hello.

•

I pass the Hi-Point every day on my way to and from the store.
    Hello, hello, hello.
    Hello, hello, hello.
    I go with empty bags, then I return with full ones, and I see this emptiness, then fullness, as reflected in these windows.
    Hello, hello.
    Hello, hello, the nothing bobs and gleams.
    Hello, hello, hello.
    Hello, hello, hello.
    I start to feel I am on the verge of knowing something new.
    I start to feel like I'm part of some strange process.

•

I leave with empty bags, then full.
    Empty, then full.
    Hello.
    The sky turns blue, then gray, but always warm-gold through the Hi-Point windows.
    You take another business trip.
    Another business trip.
    I buy a little less.
    My bags return less and less full.

•

In the morning, I watch as you sleep, as you wake, as you breathe through the space between sleeping and waking. You breathe deep, then light, as the sun starts to rise, to come in through the curtain.
A few small flakes of skin push through your chin, your cheeks.
    Small spears of hair through which your frail skin shines like broken glass.

•

I fill my bags with oranges and apples, green and red.

When I bite into them, my teeth begin to bleed.

I fill my bags with bottles of wine, red and white.

I line the empty bottles in a clumsy, green, black barricade against the door.

You take a business trip.

You take another business trip.

I buy new nylons, dangle them above my head before the light.

Imagine walking through the world on these strange, flat, legless legs.

I pass the Hi-Point, watch my gold legs shimmer.

Sad, flat, pointless gleam.

•

You take a business trip.

You take another business trip.

I take my time to get whichever ways I do not need to go.

I take my time selecting things I do not need, then buy.

Then, take them home.

I buy a new, bright blue umbrella.

Then, the sky begins to rain.

•

It rains and rains and rains. Your coffee cup sits still, now, as my finger stirs the emptiness around in it. The dregs. I feel a gentle vapidness amid these unsipped fragments, like the soils from some plant that wouldn't grow.

I wash my hands. The soap is filled with strands of hair, both mine and yours, like fine black fractures set in cool white bars of bone.

I feel my own bones, hard beneath the vagueness of their movement.

Crack the window, now, to smell the bits that rise up with the rain.

•

While you are gone—another business trip—they tear the Hi-Point down.

Day one: they break the windows into shards of glass and long, gray slabs.

Day two: they clear the innards, tubes and wire, tangled sheets and strands, soft tufts of snowy, pastel piles of insulation.

Day three: they slam into the building's metal skeleton, completing their destruction, their construction of an empty space.

I leave with empty bags.

Then full.

I stop.

I glance.

I look into the space.

My bones feel brittle and my bags feel heavy.

•

The rain clears.

You return.

The empty lot remains.

I pass the lot.

Empty, then full.

Empty, then full.

Empty, then full.

I glance at what remains, now crumbled dust.

No weeds.

No warm-lit nothing.

Bright skies.

Bigger, now.

An unreflected blue.

# SACRAMENTO

The boy's early memories are all of hospitals. White curtained windows, bright white lights, and pastel walls. He is holding green jello (his favorite) or yellowish pudding (his close second-favorite.) His mother is eating her fruit from a can. That's her favorite. She likes to eat things out of cans.

For some reason, all of the rooms contain one of two pictures. It is always a star on the beach or a foot in the sand. Both images are close-up shots with words he cannot read. He asks his mom to read them, but she doesn't answer.

She looks at him with all her tubes and bandages. Her eyes bobble up like black stones sinking down in the sand. He says, Mom, and she blinks, like his words are a dribble of water dripped down from the ceiling. Her face is a jellyfish drying up fast from the white of the sun.

•

*The woman's early memories are all of being cold. Cold feet, cold floors, cold bed, cold blankets wet with fever residue.*

*Her mother dies in winter. It is difficult to dig the grave. She watches the men. She scrapes the bits of dirt beneath her fingernails. She sees the water slowly seeping through the layers of her boots, half-wishes she could see her toes turn black.*

*It is 1847. She notates the year in her Bible. The scratch of her pen on the page is the sound of the cold. The ground looks wrong. The people, with their scarves, their faces buried. That is why she wants to move to Sacramento.*

•

The girl's early memories are all of churches. Dim rooms, windows of squares black green, brown bottle, jelly red. The pews, they smell of carpet stained with vomit-cleaning chemicals. The priest, he smells of sweat-stained polyester robes.

Her mother and her father work in factories. They look like the churches, their long windows sectioned the same.

Sometimes the whole world seems like it is framed by filtered light, and wherever she is, and wherever she goes, she feels she should be kneeling.

•

*The woman is reading her letter again. She has crumpled the crease from repeated unfolding. She stares at the letter. The letter says, hello, my love.*

*She thinks, hello, my love. She unfurls this phrase. She smoothes all its edges. Sometimes she believes she is mending the phrase, like a small bird her migrating words have abandoned. She is stroking its feathers. She's trying to help it be hers. But sometimes she is crushing the bird in her thoughts. And sometimes, she is breaking its wings.*

*The letter says, hello, my love. I am thinking of you, and when you will be with me. I am looking out onto the field where the seedlings are starting to grow. By the time you are here, all the seeds will be tall, and the seeds will be plants, and the plants will be ready. The earth and the sky and the trees will be new shades, perhaps shades that I've never seen.*

*She imagines the words like they're things she can crumple and change. She thinks, hello, my love, hello, my love, hello, my love.*

*She has never met this man. She has never seen his face. She can't imagine what his voice would sound like.*

*She feels stupid and flat when she thinks of these things, like a landscape unmarked and unwandered. A landscape you pass through. The landscape she'll cross if she's going to reach him.*

*The voice that repeats the words, hello, my love, is not his, or how she would imagine his voice. The voice that repeats the words, hello, my love, is her own.*

•

His recent memories are all of beer cans stacked in towers. All the tower stacks have been arranged around a ragged army tent. It's like his mother tried to make a fortress. He admires that. He wishes it weren't such a stupid fortress.

Every day, he wakes up, gets up, and descends the basement steps. He's careful not to knock the rows of towered beer cans. It's difficult because they take up almost every inch of space. He has carved out a delicate pathway that seems to get thinner and thinner each time.

He says, Mom. He hears a wheezing little groan inside the tent.

He says, Mom.

She says, what do you want? But she doesn't emerge.

He says, Mom, he called today. What should I tell him?

She groans and she rustles around. She says, I don't know. Tell him that I'm dying. I am dying. Soon I will be dead.

He climbs the stairs back to his room and he looks at himself in the mirror. He thinks, I look fat, and he takes off his clothing to check. He looks back in the mirror. He thinks, yeah, I am totally fat. His stomach rolls are almost on the verge of drooping. He fixes his hair. There is still hope, he thinks, if I do something now. He thinks, I need a girlfriend. I just need a really nice girlfriend.

He tries to imagine a girl who would want to date him. He doesn't want to think she would be fat, like him. He doesn't want to learn to like his fat, or someone else's. He thinks, maybe she'd be thin, but kinda weird. He imagines a girl with smooth hair and a pretty complexion. Then, he mentally tangles her hair and adds zits, scabs, and make-up. He imagines her wearing a black mini-skirt and black fishnets with black lace-up boots. He thinks, yeah, that's his favorite, but then he feels stupid again. So he pictures her wearing black jeans and a dark zip-up jacket, his close second-favorite. He thinks, yeah, that's more realistic, and he feels proud of himself.

•

*The woman decides what to bring on her long trip west. She doesn't know how many miles lie between them. She knows she must pack light. She knows she'll have to cross a desert. She knows that she won't see him til she reaches Sacramento.*

*She packs her quilt, her Bible, and her diary. She packs her sewing needles and her knives. She takes a picture off the mantle, places it aside. She fingers through some less-used pieces of embroidery.*

*The woman looks out of her window. The morning is wet, cold, and gray, and the streets are deserted. The mud-paved road is thick and treacherous. The rooftops of the houses drip with melting snow. The church steeple points like a finger misguiding its followers.*

•

She tries to imagine her boyfriend. She hasn't seen him in 6 weeks. It's 11 pm on a week night, too late to be walking alone, not asleep. She is tired of chewing her lip in the dark. She opens the fridge and the pantry. No food. She slides on her shoes and she shrugs on her shirt and her jacket.

She creaks the screen door and she opens her bag. She digs deep for her last cigarette. It is torn and tobacco has spilt from the tip, but she lights it up anyway.

A dark little pool of summertime sounds paints her memory black. The purr of insects, distant cars, and other things that do not matter. It's inviting, to be overwhelmed by all these sounds that do not matter. More inviting than the constant non sound of not him not there.

She's walking along the periphery of town, where all the neighborhoods turn into factories and industrial parks. The industrial parks are surrounded by trees that don't seem to know why they are there. She pokes through the trees like she'll find something. She doesn't find anything.

She calls him again. She knows he won't like it, but she doesn't care. She has to call three times before he answers. When he does, there is a pause before he speaks. Her ear fills with the crackled gauze of other people talking.

He says, hey, what's up?
She says, not that much.
He says, are you ok?
She says, yeah, sure. Are you ok?
He says, I'm fine. I'm at a party.
She says, where?
In Sacramento, he says.
She says, where is that?
He says, I don't know. I should go now.
She says, please wait. Can't you talk for just another minute?
He says, why, is something wrong?

She thinks about it for a moment. She thinks, maybe. Probably, there is.

She stares into that patch of pointless trees. She pulls off a branch and she breaks it up into her hand. She scatters the twigs and the pieces of bark and she opens and closes her fingers. She blows off the dirt from the palm of her hand and she thinks, maybe this is my wish.

She pictures all the trees that stand between them. She imagines a time without highways or paved roads or cars to cut swiftly through spaces. She imagines a time without telephone wires or invisible sound waves of distance.

She thinks of how much more it meant then, two people apart, or together. She wonders, do the trees absorb the years of sounds unspoken?

He says, hey, is something wrong? Are you still there? Are you still there?

Am I still there? She wonders. Where is there? She doesn't know.

He says, are you still there? She thinks, I'm not. She doesn't answer. He says, please don't call me if you have nothing to say.

I'm sorry, she says.

He says, have a good night.

She says, have a good night. Then, his voice is gone.

•

*She sets out with a heavy wagon and a heavy stomach. Her footsteps feel heavy too, a little bit ridiculous. She wonders when she'll start to feel hungry. She wonders when she'll wonder why she chose to bring these things.*

*When they get to the river, the men take control of the wagons. She walks through the river. The water comes up to her waist. Her skirt billows out so she can't see her feet or the way they are moving. A part of her worries she'll drift to the edge and discover her feet have been carried away.*

*Her feet emerge slick with the slime of the river. She looks up at the sky. The sky is gray and white. The grass is brown. The whole world smells like damp dead grass and wet warm breath of animals. She walks beside the oxen and she wonders what they're thinking.*

•

They meet at party. She's wearing his favorite, which is funny. She doesn't normally wear things like mini-skirts and fishnets. She's trying to be sexy for the party.

She thinks about her boyfriend at some house in Sacramento. She thinks of all the cute girls who must be there. She pictures them in something like she's wearing. She pictures their flat bodies and flat-ironed hair. Their breasts are little exclamation points. Their bodies end their phrases with so much exuberance.

She doesn't know why she is there. He doesn't know why he is there. They are in a basement standing by the band. The band members are dancing, but basically no one is dancing. The lead singer sings like he's trying to make himself puke.

This is bullshit, he says. He is standing beside her.

She nods in response.

I mean all of this, he says, to clarify.

She says, yeah, I think you're right. They leave.

He wants to tell her he thinks she is pretty. He wants to tell her he likes what she's wearing. He wants to say, I can't believe how much you are my favorite. Her breasts look big and round and serious.

He drinks from the 40 he stole from his mom. He says, want some?

She takes it and drinks.

He says, sometimes I wonder how long it will take for my body to fully decay.

That depends on a lot, she says absently. That all depends on the body, the place where it's buried. The temperature, climate. The age of the person. The state of his organs. The strength of his bones.

I don't think I would last very long in the ground, he says, reaching to her for the 40.

She looks over his body. She thinks, no, you probably wouldn't.

He walks her home. She doesn't feel like sleeping when she gets there. So they wander awhile, past the pointless trees and factories. The night is humid. All around, the smell of soil stains the air. The factories groan, and the leaves of the pointless trees whisper.

I don't have any friends, he says, tossing the 40 aside.

I don't have any either, she says, just my boyfriend. He's always on tour.

Let's be friends, he says, suddenly. She looks up, stunned by his words. How strange to hear a person's need spelled out so plainly.

Okay, sure, she says, and she smiles unsurely. He smiles a smile of relief. I don't know what to do now, she says. Should I hug you? Or what?

I could go for a hug, he admits. So she hugs him. The hug lasts three seconds. He counts in his head. When she steps back, the smell of her fruit-scented hair product lingers.

You smell like green jello, he says.

She says, that's good to know.

They stand for awhile, not speaking. They've said all they needed to say.

He goes home and pulls out a freezer-burned dinner and nukes it and carries it down to the basement. He puts it in front of the tent. He has to set it on the floor.

His mother says, you smell like you've been with a girl.

He says, I'm moving out. I need my own space.

She coughs. Well, go figure. Well, I'm dying anyway.

He says, I'm dying too. I just get sick of watching.

•

*A man sits by her by the fire when they camp. He is older, unmarried. He is strong and broad-shouldered, but quiet. He clears his throat and offers her some water. The shadows make his full gray beard seem dark, like looming mountains.*

*She says, thank you. She drinks.*

*He says, full moon. He drinks, but from a bottle.*

*She says, so it is. She looks at the moon, which is full, like a boil or blister. She looks at his profile, the glaze of his skin from the fire. His cheeks are flushed, but hollowed out. He sighs.*

*Her stomach aches with unfamiliarity. She's hungry. She no longer feels heavy. She is aching with the urge to fill her hunger. She is aching with the urge to feel full.*

*He says, best keep an eye peeled, when the moon is full.*

*She says, so I've been told. The moon makes me afraid.*

*He stares up like his eyes have been pulled open by the sky. Best keep an eye peeled, ma'am, he says, if you know what I mean.*

•

The next night, he returns to her front door. She isn't there, so he waits for her out on the front porch. He waits for two hours. The air from the porch is refreshing. He likes where she lives. It is nice to be sort of inside of her house, but not really.

He likes it because porches are the opposite of fortresses. He could live on this porch if she let him. He wonders why most people don't live on porches.

When she gets home, she jumps when she sees him. She says, what the fuck.

He says, I'm sorry. I just felt so lonely.

He starts to leave, but she says, no, ok, wait, it's ok. Let's just walk awhile. I still don't feel like going in, she says.

They walk that night. They walk again the next night. It becomes a nightly thing. He brings two bottles wrapped in paper bags.

They drink until the fields feel immense. They laugh at things they do not think are funny. They walk until it seems like they could walk across the borders of one state into the next into the next.

•

*The days grow warm and long, which means more walking. The sameness of the landscape hypnotizes her. The roses of her calico look faded. They have turned from golden green to pale flax to grayish white.*

*She has $40 left, but she won't need it. They will live on honey, fruit, and fresh new vegetables. She will not need these boxes of dried bread, these strips of salted meat. She will not need to pickle everything she picks.*

*The days grow warm and long, but she grows frightened of the nights. The darkness deafens her to all but sounds that should be threatening. She folds her hands and clutches at her heart. She thinks of when she'll have to share his bed. She wonders if she'll sleep with him. She wonders if she'll sleep. Perhaps she'll lie awake each night, in fear beside him.*

•

One night, he admits he's a virgin. He says this when asked how he lost his virginity. He says, still got it. He hurls a 40. He wishes that he had a shotgun to shoot it.

I lost mine when I was 16, she says. I was out drinking with friends in the woods. I went to swim in the lake, and some guy was already there, pissing. I looked at his dick. I was drunk and I wanted to see it. We went and we fucked in the back of his car. It didn't seem fair to say no

How was his dick? He asks.

It was so-so, she says. Kind of dry. It was shaped like a mushroom.

That sounds really gross, he says, softly. His own dick is hard.

Speak for yourself, she says. I'm not a virgin, at least.

There's a silence they fill up by digging around for more beer.

So, why are you a virgin? She asks him. They look at the ground and continue to wander. The ground is long dry yellow grass that is buzzing with crickets. It whispers and crackles beneath them.

He says, I don't know. Never met anyone that I liked enough.

She smiles a weird misshapen smile. But you like me though, right?

He looks back at her and he doesn't smile. He thinks about it for a moment. He says, right.

•

*The days grow warmer, longer. They keep getting lost. They circle. She hums to herself. Birds circle them as they approach the desert.*

*This is the last river, they tell her. There will be no more, before the desert. You must take on all the water that you can.*

*She cups the water in her hands to drink it. She cups her hands around her stomach, bulging up with water. She tells her stomach, you can make it, like she's talking to a child that will die a little with each step she takes.*

*This is the last river, they tell her. You must retrain yourself, from here. Your body must change now, learn how not to want all the things that it needs.*

•

He gets his own apartment on the edge of town, where things are cheap. He's going to make his home among the pointless trees and factories. Each hour, he can hear the bell tone of the changing shift. He wonders if that's how he'll come to count his days.

His apartment looks just like a one-hour motel that's been repainted white again thousands of times. When he thinks of this, he thinks, that totally is what it is.

He thinks, I need to get some shit before I go insane. I need to get some shit that girls would like. Specifically, his favorite girl. Some shit for her.

He goes to the thrift store and mills around. He touches things and smells them. What shit do girls like? He has no idea. He thinks they like blankets and flowers. He picks up a blanket with flowers and smells it. The flowers smell like cigarettes and oatmeal.

He picks up a framed antique landscape and looks at the image. Leaves of blackish green are climbing up the set of sandstone pillars. They are sheathed in rays of sunlight that seems strangely hesitant. The hills beneath the pillars—not the stones—seem to be crumbling.

Meanwhile, his mother's bottle drops and shatters. In her mind, she is a picture in a frame. She has picked herself out as a photograph, glossy, age 26, hair streaming down. She is laughing. She's hugging some flowers. Here, she is her favorite.

•

*To make room for the water, she tosses her candles and candlesticks.*
*To make room for the water, she tosses her spindles and spinning wheel.*
*To make room for the water, she tosses her grandfather clock.*
*To make room for the water, she tosses her grandmother's china.*
*To make room for the water, she tosses her boxes of beads.*
*To make room for the water, she tosses her hope chest of lace.*
*To make room for the water, she tosses her flour, her bread, meat, and vegetables.*
*To make room for the water, she tosses her silverware. Now she must eat with her hands.*
*To make room for the water, she tosses her mirror. She shudders when it shatters.*
*Now, she'll wake every morning and wash without seeing her face. She thinks, it's for the best. She knows she's giving up on something.*

•

It has been a whole week since she's heard from her boyfriend. She calls then hangs up five times in ten minutes. He calls her back and answers, what the fuck?

Sorry, she says. This is off to a bad start, like always. I just, you know, wondered, you know, how you were doing.

I'm doing fine, he says.

Oh, she says. I'm doing fine as well.

Jesus, he says.

What's the matter? She says.

Nothing, he says. I'm doing fine.

She pauses. I miss you, she says. But does she really?

A pause. Don't you miss me? She says. She thinks he doesn't.

His voice softens. Of course, yeah, he says. Yeah, I miss you.

So what are you doing? She asks.

I don't know. Nothing, really. He pauses. Nothing much.

Anything fun? She says.

No, he says, no. Nothing much. Nothing fun. Nothing anything.

Don't you want to know what I've been doing? She says.

No, not really, he says. I mean, no. I mean, no, well, you know, like, I mean, like, I think I can guess.

He pauses, as though to absorb the jagged tone of his own answer. She can hear a motorcycle passing through the line between them. He says, sometimes, I just wish I could hold you. Wish we didn't have to talk like this.

She thinks, we don't.

He says, babe, I'm sorry.

She is calling on a walk along the factories, of course. The branches of the pointless trees are moaning. Somewhere hidden in their depths are silent birds. She thinks about the birds and all the bugs within their feathers.

And the bugs in the feathers.

And the feathers in the birds.

And the birds in the branch.

And the branch in the tree.

And the tree in the hole.

And the hole in the ground.

He doesn't like to talk, she thinks. He doesn't like to talk. She recycles this phrase a few times in her head like she's stupid. He doesn't like to talk, she thinks. He doesn't like to talk. With each repeat, the muscles in her throat clench tighter, tighter. She swallows and her chest begins to feel concave.

And the bugs in the feathers.

And the feathers in the birds.
And the birds in the branch.
And the branch in the tree.
And the tree in the hole.
And the hole in the ground.
And the green grass grows all around.

By the 8th repeat and tighten, she can't swallow anymore. She can't clench any further. She unclenches and explodes.

No, she says. You know what. No. I think that's fucking bullshit.

Through the phone, she hears his fingers drumming on a table. She hears the drumming stop and knows they're rising to his temples. Jesus Christ, she hears him say. Are you nuts? I didn't do anything.

I think I'm breaking up with you, she hears herself say. He says something back, but for some reason she can't hear him.

•

*An elderly woman in the train is ill. She is coughing as she walks until she falls. The men fold her up into blankets and make her a nest in the back of her wagon.*

*The moon is full. The wind is heavy, and the night is strangely cold.*

*She lies awake and hears the woman coughing. Somewhere near, she hears another woman crying to her husband.*

*They unwrap the woman's body in the morning. Her face is covered in a rash of sores. The men exchange looks. One man takes off his hat. They say, just try to get as much rest as you can.*

•

One night, he's too lonely to wait for her any longer. He imagines what she smells like, in those fishnets. He sits on her porch until she shows up. He still doesn't have her number.

He sits on her porch and he drinks. When she shows up, he's drunk.

He says, I don't like it, you know. The fact that I'm a virgin.

She says, yes, I know. I wouldn't like it either.

I'm a virgin because I don't like myself, he says.

She says, I don't know if I like myself or not.

He says, I have a new apartment. Do you want to see it?

She thinks for a moment about what he's really asking.

I bought a new painting, he says. It reminds me of you.

They stand in silence for another moment while she thinks.

His ears prick. What's that clicking sound? He says.

She is sliding the cap of her lipstick around in her pocket. Oh, nothing, she tells him. She takes the lipstick out and puts it on.

You look pretty, he says.

She says, thank you. She looks in the hand mirror.

You always look pretty, he says.

She glares into the mirror. She almost snaps. Instead, she starts to cry. I'm not, she says. I'm not. I'm not. I'm not.

He pulls her to his chest with a resolve that startles both of them. He holds her and he stares into the distance. It takes him so much time to process what he's doing that he doesn't even hear her when she says, um, you can touch me.

She repeats, you can touch me, and he does.

He touches her hair.

He touches her chin.

He touches her neck.

He touches her shoulders.

He touches the lengths of her arms, which are naked and soft.

His fingers move around her wrists in small repeating circles. She looks up at him. His dick feels like a dead fish on a spear. He needs to burn this feeling. He says, let's go back to my apartment.

She says, okay. Let's go. Then her voice gets really gentle. He doesn't like how she sounds like another person.

They take the indoor staircase, which is deep red brown-stained carpet. In between each door there is a bright green shell-shaped sconce of light. She says, this hall is creepy in a good way, like a church. He thinks she doesn't really sound convinced.

He opens the door, which is also green, flicks on the light. The apartment is basically empty inside. There's a painting and four cardboard boxes. In the corner there's a pillow and a folded sleeping bag. He doesn't have a bed to sleep on yet.

She points at it. Doesn't sleeping like that hurt your back?

He says, no, it doesn't, but it does. He doesn't care.

He thinks of how he doesn't care. It makes his dick feel better. He steps back and he sits, then lies back on the pillow.

She says, should I lie down on there with you? He says, no. When she's close, his dick feels like it's scraping down a plastic slide. He doesn't like the fear of getting shocked and being thus exposed. He says, no. You stand there, if that's all right.

Okay, she says. Should I, you know, do something?

He thinks, then he breathes in. He says, yes.

What should I do first? She says. She is looking down.

He says, first take off your shirt. He's looking at her.

She takes it off and folds it on the floor, just like his sleeping bag. She folds her arms across her bra. She says, it's cold.

It isn't cold, he says.

She moves her arms back to her sides. She says, oh. I guess it really isn't.

He breathes in again. He says, take off your bra.

She takes it off and folds it by the shirt. Her breasts look like two frozen teardrops made of milk.

Her nipples are so light they almost blend into the rest of her. He wants to watch her touch them til they turn the shade they should be.

He says, nice. That sounds so creepy, he says, sorry.

She says, that's okay. What should I do now?

He says, touch your nipples. She brushes her fingers against them. He says, pinch them, but their color doesn't change.

He says, take your skirt off. She takes off her skirt. She's wearing cotton panties with a faded yellow rose print. He says, take your panties off. She takes them off. Her pubic hair is trimmed and shaved into a strip. He doesn't think he likes the way that looks. He didn't think she was the sort of girl who shaved that way.

He says, let me see your lips. He breathes. He says, I mean your pussy. She shifts her heels, adjusts her legs a bit. She parts her lips and holds them open, one hand on each side. She looks at her toenails and thinks of how she needs to trim them.

He says, wow, and she thinks of her boyfriend, her ex-boyfriend. She thinks about how she would never be thinking with him. She thinks how he'd be there, then inside her. She thinks of how sometimes he would be finished up already.

She says, should I take your clothes off?

He says, just take off my pants. His dick smells like strawberry mousse and it looks like pink play dough.

She says, are you hard?

He doesn't look. He says, um, I think so.

She says, should I suck it?

He says, I don't know.

There is a moment of silence. She looks at his dick and she almost gives up and gets dressed. Instead, she undresses the rest of his body and presses her skin to his skin and she closes her eyes as she wiggles around on his lap as she's trying to fuck him.

•

*By the time they reach the desert, she is feverish. Many people in the train now share the woman's rash. She scratches at her face. Her lips are cracked. She cannot drink. She cannot rinse her hands or wash the sand stuck to her skin.*

*She sees the carcasses of animals that other trains have left behind. Birds peck the sundried bones of mules and horses. If I die, she thinks, they'll leave me in the sun. She imagines a bird with the bead of her eye bleeding into its beak.*

*The bright sky bleaches out the earth. The cloudless sky looks white. The world is filled with long dark rifts that scream for rain to fill them. There's a haze on the horizon. She keeps seeing mounds. She wonders if they're bodies. Yes, of course. Of course they're bodies.*

*Bone pierced linens, shards of meatless ribs and emptied sacks, splayed ringless fingers, legs and hipbones, no meat in between them.*

*Someone's dog or just a dog is digging in the sand. It digs until it stops to leave a stream of red-stained urine. The piss stream trickles into shapes like stalks of wheat. She smiles. She thinks, that's what hope is, noticing these things.*

•

She goes home and she goes straight to her bedroom. She digs through her dresser drawers until she finds his shirt. She carries it to bed. She strokes the buttons on its wrists. She plucks at the embroidered flowers. She fingers the frays of its ribboned lapels.

The shirt says, sorry. I just don't know what to say.

She tells it, that's ok. You're just a shirt. Just let me hold you.

The shirt says, it feels strange to just be held. To not be worn. It feels like you're trying to make me something I'm not.

She closes her eyes and she ponders its words for a moment. It seems sinister, making things into things that they are not. Is she sinister? No. Is she doing this? Yes. She says, seriously, what if I am?

The shirt sighs and it says, okay. It curls up in her arms. The shirt smells like stale weed, warm bread, and boy's deodorant. The remnants of his odors smell like shirt, but not like him. The shirt smells her and wishes it could turn into a man.

•

*She holds the letter in her tent at night. She holds the letter and she reads it in her head. Her thoughts are just mirages. She ignores them. She ignores this. She repeats, hello, my love, hello, my love, hello, my love.*

*She imagines he doesn't exist. She imagines she doesn't exist. She imagines these words as a soft bluish vapor that quenches her pain to the core.*

•

He leaves his new apartment. He goes home. He tiptoes down the stairs and crawls into the tent.

He curls into his mother's arms. She's sleeping and he knows that she is dreaming about being someone else he doesn't know.

He tells her, I love you.
She tells him, I love you too.
He shuts his eyes. He pretends that the tent is surrounded by stars.

# IN FULL VIEW

This used to be the peep show, says the manager. She walks me through the attic of the club. The halls are lined with mirrors, like a a dim-lit sexual Versailles. Red wires of lights appear to make my movements glow.

It's storage now. She taps a naked mannequin. Brown boxes tower up against the booths. The doors are sectioned off with pinkish metal bars, like corral stalls for unused carousels.

She walks me through a locked-in dressing room. You'll be in Booth 3, she says, opening the last in a line of white doors. She hands me a bottle of spray and a roll of paper towels. She shows me how to put my pin into the booth control box.

The curtain comes up when they put in the money, she says.

I nod. When does it come down?

She says, when you push this button.

When do I push the button? I ask, tugging on my earring.

She says, push the button when the show is finished.

•

The peep show is said to originate from a traveling toy theater. These performances were known as raree shows. Children would gather to gaze into holes in wood boxes. Inside of these boxes were images, slides controlled by an unseen pull string.

The images did not move until the string was pulled. They were narrated with spoken stories from their traveling host. Sometimes, the narrator would dance or play with puppets for the children. He would charge them extra to look through the holes.

Often, the pictures told stories that were partially familiar, fairy tales or famous operas and epics. The narrator shortened these stories and whittled them down into simpler language. The narrator altered these stories so his customers could understand.

•

I watch the mirror put on my face. My features take their form. My eyes become two heavy lidded fronds of blackish lace. I look and think, what sort of person am I? Then, my mouth becomes a pair of lips that do not need to say.

A man wanders into my booth and he fumbles around with his wallet. So, um, how does this work? He says, muffled behind the glass.

The curtain comes up when you put in the money, I tell him.

He says, oh. He puts the money in. The curtain rises.

I say, good morning.

He says, hi.

I ask him, how are you?

He says, fine.

I say, you're my first customer.

Oh. He nods and makes a terse little sound that is not quite a laugh or a cough. So, um, can you explain? What kind of show do you do?

I pretend I know the answer to his question. I can do any show you would like, I say. Whatever that means. Is there anything special you'd like for me to do today?

He shrugs. Just want to watch you take your clothes off. He laugh coughs. And to maybe see your asshole.

I turn around slowly and gaze at a light that my customer cannot see. I shimmy around as I slide down my bra straps, unclasp, and unveil my tits. I turn to face him with my arm positioned so he can't quite see them. Then, I lower my arm, slowly, and look toward his face.

He says, very nice. I can't see his face, but I can tell he's nodding. From waist up, my customer's body is a shadowed silhouette. From waist down, he is illuminated with theatrical contrast. A pair of dark pants. A leather belt. Three buttons of a light blue blouse.

I ask what he would like for me to take off next. He says, take off your panties. Leave the garter belt and stockings. I remove them and pretend to toss my hair to see him better, but I'm really looking up into the light. I feel him nodding again. I ask, what would you like to happen, now? The light says, please lean back and spread your legs.

•

I never really played with dolls when I was little. I pretended with my friends, but that was for their benefit. I didn't understand the point. It creeped me out to watch them play. I didn't like their voices, making words for mouths that did not move.

When alone, I would arrange my dolls in still lives. I'd dress them up and set the scene just right. A bright blue scarf became the ocean. A marled wool tie became the dock. A bag of slivered almonds opened and became the beach.

I positioned the dolls in their natural setting and snapped photos on a disposable camera. I maintained the photos in albums, but I never looked at them. I knew the dolls weren't real, and the pictures didn't make them real. The fact of their existence was enough.

•

The sounds around the booth tell stories of the things I cannot see. The manager making her lunch. She is hungry. The microwave opens before the clock beeps. The janitor making his rounds. He is tired. He yawns. The other girls. Customers stopping to talk at the first or the second booth.

Hello. How are you? Would you like a show?

It's a mutual masturbation show. It's $20.

It's for 10 minutes. $20 is 10 minutes.

Okay. Step up around the door. I'll be there soon.

The sound of fake orgasms. *Ah, ah, ah.* Some from real girls, some from recordings. There's another hall next to my booth where the men can watch videos.

A man comes to my booth. He pays. The curtain rises. I take off my clothes. He says, your breasts. My wife, she used to look like you.

Does she know that you come to the show? I ask. He nods. It keeps me out of too much trouble, he explains.

As he's coming, he presses his left hand up into the glass. His hand stands out clearly against the blur of his foreshortened frame. I lean in. My reflected features sharpen. My face blends in with the shadowed outlines of this stranger's body.

•

One weekend, I saw my dad watching a film with Halle Berry. I don't recall which film it was, but it was dumb. I said, Dad, this film is dumb. He nodded. Yeah.

She's hot though, Halle Berry, said my dad. I squinted like he'd given me a strange new math equation. I didn't understand the math of Dad + Halle Berry. I didn't understand the sum of two such different parts.

I looked at Halle Berry in her midriff shirt, her skin-tight jeans. My mother was her opposite in every way. I didn't know you felt like that, I said. I felt like I'd forgiven him for something.

I wanted to know what my father thought about, in secret. Later on that evening, in my room, I googled

*Halle Berry, nude.*

•

A thin young man approaches the booth. His movements are quivery. He peers into the glass like he's parting a thick mesh of branches. He mouths like a goldfish, some words I cannot hear. I motion toward the hall phone, but he doesn't understand my gesture.

I wave him toward me. I write on a sheet of paper, *$20 for 10 minutes*. I hold the paper in front of the window. He nods.

The curtain goes up. He stands before me, fully clothed. I ask, what can I do for you today?

He pulls something up on his cell phone and types something into it. He holds the screen up to the window. The text says, *sexy*.

I nod, assuming *sexy* means *I'll have the usual*. I give him the usual. I turn to show off that I'm wearing a backless dress. I slide down the dress, then slide it up to show my stockings.

He still isn't doing anything. I stop. Is something wrong? I ask. Is this not what you wanted?

He types into his phone again and holds it up. *Sexy nude live girl.*

I start to take off my dress. He shakes his head. He types, *live real girl. I want you. I want real live girl sex.*

I don't think I can give you what you're looking for, I tell him. He keeps typing. *I want real live. Real live girl sex.*

In confusion or desperation, he pounds his head into the glass. I push the button and the curtain closes. This show's finished. I can hear him pounding from behind the curtain. I'm not paid enough to be a real live girl.

•

I was 19 the first time a partner told me I was sexy. At least, that was the first time I recall now. My boyfriend at the time had split with me the night before. We'd had an argument. I'd packed a bag and left.

I was walking toward a party that was near his house. I'd dressed up too much for the party. I knew I was going to his house instead. I wore a slim black dress, fishnets, and shiny heeled shoes. There was nowhere else for me to go, looking like that.

It was a cool autumn night, the kind that smells like smoke. The dead leaves chattered secretively in their branches. I knocked on his door, and he looked up and down when he answered. Going somewhere special? Going to a party, I replied.

He poured me a glass of red wine from the bottle he'd had sitting out. He handed it to me like maybe, when I took it, I would disappear. I sat beside him on the couch. I sipped the wine and spaced out. He said, don't drink too much wine before the party.

I put my hand on his leg. He sighed. He said, look. We can't do this. But, he sighed again, a different sigh, you are extremely sexy.

I left his house after I finished my wine glass. I went to the party. I looked out of place, but most people were too drunk to notice. The people were dancing, so I danced. I was not a good dancer. I was not good at moving and doing things in my dress.

A young man with asymmetrical hair started dancing with me. He got really close right away, like he knew what the dress I was wearing was for. He whispered, I live in this house. We could go to my bedroom. We did. Inside his bedroom, I went down on him.

He murmured from above me in an almost monotone, like he was reading from a poorly written script. *You like sucking that cock, you slut. You like sucking that big cock.* I nodded, but he didn't seem to care. *You like sucking that cock, you whore, don't you. You like that cock. You like to suck that cock. You like to suck that cock.*

I had no lines in this script about whores sucking cocks. His words began to blur together from their repetition.

*Suckthatcockyouliketosucktha*
*tfuckingcockyouliketofuckingssuckthatfuck*
*ingcockyouliketosuckthatcockyoufuckingslut.*

He came in my mouth and his come tasted faintly of urine. We looked at each other like, well, now, whatever just happened is finished.

I went to the bathroom and looked in the mirror. What sort of person am I? I imagined my ex-boyfriend's sigh. *You are extremely sexy.*

•

As a liminal space, the peep show draws attention to its script. It is clear what cannot happen in this play. There is a glass wall and a curtain that defines when it begins and ends. The curtain writes the play that is performed.

You cannot touch, you cannot smell, you cannot taste. You cannot view of me what I do not reveal. You cannot move my body without asking me to move it. Language is movement, in the peep show. Your words are what you see.

By the time the curtain rises, the men usually have their cocks out. I say *men* because a woman has never come into my peep show.

The men know they have a certain space of time to get themselves off. If their goal is to *get off*. It always is, though.

•

A middle-aged man buys a show. He is tall with square-shaped shoulders. When the curtain rises, he is standing very close-up to the glass. He is so tall his face and shoulders are completely shadowed. He says, have a lot of other guys been here today?

I say, yes.

He says, how many?

I say, 6 or 7.

You lose track of them, he says.

I nod. Sometimes it's back to back.

He says, so a lot of guys came here. The men in the peep show repeat themselves, frequently. A lot of guys came in this room, with their hard dicks out.

I nod. I start to fiddle with my bra straps. I can tell that he wants to keep talking to himself throughout the show.

A lot of guys looked at those tits with their hard dicks out.

A lot of guys stroked their hard dicks while they looked at that pussy.

A lot of guys came in this room, with you there, with their hard dicks.

*Hard dicks* appears to be his preferred nomenclature.

When I'm fully nude, I ask, what would you like to happen, now? He says, lie down. I lie down on my side. No, not like that, he says. I want you to lie with your head tilted back, and your legs spread apart, like I'm standing above, and you're sucking my hard dick.

I position my body this way. His cock is looming right above me. It's veiny, which makes it look vaguely ferocious, like the ribcage of a starving dog. I close my eyes. Open your eyes, he demands. Stick your tongue out. As I start to, the sight sets him over the edge, and he comes.

I want to do that with you, he says. Can I take you out to dinner?

*Can I buy you drinks?*

*Can I give you some tips?*

*Can I buy a dress for you to wear to see me?*
*Can I pay for a different performance? This one finished so quickly.*

•

Even though we're engaged for 10 minutes of time (it's *time*; I make no promises,) most men who approach me desire to make some connection. Some men simply want to control me and don't like the fact that the curtain goes down. Some men are simply lonely and they want a more long-term companion.

Sometimes, I feel uneasy with the imbalance. Though my experiences vary, my gain from them—*money*— is clear. The takeaway gain for my customers is more ambiguous. What do they feel? And how long does it last?

•

A stooped elderly man approaches the booth. He stumbles as he walks. He is wearing a shirt that says *Special Olympics 2000*. He presses his face against the glass. He has no teeth. I look up at the light and ask it, how are you today?

You are beautiful, says the light.

I tell it, thank you.

Could you please take off your clothes? It asks politely.

I do, and as I'm doing so, I see his cock, which he has also pressed right up against the glass.

You're beautiful, the light says. Then, it whispers, you are perfect. You are perfect. I'm in love with you. I love you.

I say nothing in response. I try to fill the time. The light breathes. I don't owe him. The light breathes. I don't know what I'm worth.

# THE INTERVIEW

She hears the cars pass, distantly, a soft, consistent rhythm. She breathes through her nose. Her chest rises as they approach. She lets her breath release in time with each departure. She is breathing as the highway breathes, a set of cold, gray, concrete lungs.

She is playing a game, lying by herself, there, in her bed.

It is only a game in the sense that there are rules.

She needs rules, or else she'd be lying in bed, doing nothing.

She hates doing nothing, but she doesn't know what to do.

The object of the game is just to lie as still as possible. The object sounds much simpler than it is. Now, for example, drops of rain begin to tap against the window, and she really, really, really has to pee.

Rule #1: Keep your eyes closed.

Rule #2: Breathe slow, light breaths.

Rule #3: Lie on your back, legs straight, arms flat against your sides.

Rule #4: Listen for all the different sounds outside the room.

Rule #5: Blend them inside your head until they merge into one sound.

She is allowed to use her mind in any way she needs as long as she's not thinking of her life, but using it to play the game. She reaches out her mental spiderwebs of softly blinking energy and gathers all the sounds that she is hearing.

The raindrops tapping on the glass into the metal pipes into the tunneled channels of the highway's respiration funneling into her own, slow, even breathing, bursts of tendrils in her mind, white noise she stirs into the vague direction of these sounds.

She gathers all these sounds into a low, reverberating pressure, wraps it round her bladder like a ghostly ribbon made of thought. She breathes in and her bladder twitches. She breathes out. Her bladder hums. She breathes in deep. Her bladder stiffens. She breathes out. Her bladder moans.

Her stomach starts to growl. She tries to gather up this sound. Her stomach doesn't listen and a wisp of piss releases.

She thinks, shit. Okay. I guess I lose this game, this time. Again.
She opens up her eyes and squints against the light.
She shifts her legs.
She sits up, sits there, leaning over, on the edge.
She stares down at the ground.
She stares down at her feet.
She stares into the dirty, sandy colored carpet, swallowing her dull, empty anticipation of an ocean wave.

•

Her phone rings and she answers.
She can hear the ocean, softly, in the background, pressing up against her ear.
She strains to hear it, but her mother starts to speak.
She loses track.
She cannot listen to her mother and the ocean.
Hello, mom.
I remembered.
Yeah, the interview.
I know.
Of course.
I know. I know.
The black blouse and the gray skirt.
Yeah, they're clean.
For just a moment, she can hear the ocean seeping through the phone.
A wave, particularly strong, comes crashing to the shore.
No, I remembered.
No, I know.
I know. I know.
I won't forget.
No, I remembered.

Yes, of course.
I won't forget.
She hears a bird call through phone, three times.
She shuts her eyes.
I won't forget.
I won't forget.
I won't forget.

•

She runs the shower water til the steam fogs up the mirror. She steps into the shower and she pisses down the drain. She spits a string of drool into the stream of steaming piss. She tilts her face into the water, coughs, and clears her throat.

She feels clear. She feels clean. She feels okay.

She bends down at the waist to shave her legs. She looks down at the long array of blonde nubs set in black holes in her skin. She thinks of black holes in her body.

She towels herself off, brushes her teeth. She towels off a little circle window in the fogged up mirror. She studies herself in this circle: white foamed mouth, wet brown hair. She shakes off her head to dry her hair. She thinks, mad dog, mad dog.

•

She thinks, eye contact, eye contact. She looks across the room. She's looking at a woman not much older than herself. The woman interviewing her has clean, blonde, upswept hair. The woman's lips are pressed into a long thin line.

The long white strips of light blink over small tan squares of ceiling over long gray planes of cubicles of light gray faded carpet over black and white text posters over brown flecked squares of carpet over windows of translucent green tinged glass.

She blinks.

The woman's long thin lips are twitching slightly.

She attempts to smile.

The woman looks at her like she is doing something wrong.

This is the place you get, the room you get, the woman that you get when you fill out an online form to be a Service Specialist.

The woman interviewer asks about her favorite things.

She clears her throat. She says something generic like, keeping things organized.

The woman interviewer asks where she will be, five years from now.

Right here, she says. She looks into the woman's cold blue eyes.

The woman interviewer asks, what is your greatest strength?

She says, my greatest strength is staying focused on one thing for a long time.

What is your greatest weakness? Asks the woman interviewer.

I don't know, she says, still focused on the woman's cold blue eyes.

She takes a typing test. She types the lines of lightly flashing words inside a little paragraph inside a blinking box:

Dates drier ills erosion! Oil codes will stand in come to cease the Leakage! Dares accumulation follow actor mild curl? Coil found erasing solar moon aloft cruel crooked idols: begin answer, enter, insert inert people, sacred sounds around! Cool moons cold rivers found and corked the ribbon caskets open closing, soil softened lofts erode now follow stand alone no more.

Her fingers curl now, twitching, as the cold blue woman tells her time is up. The woman nods and blinks. She tells her, thank you for your time.

Then, just before she leaves, the woman says, I like your coat.

The woman says this quickly, like she has to get it out.

Thank you, she says.

The woman looks down.

She looks down.

It is a lovely color, says the woman.

Lovely, ocean blue.

•

She walks home, then, beneath the cool moon, the cold light rivulets reflected in oil puddles in the streets that gleam with Leakage!

 She gets home, looks down at the city that is growing in the sink. Pillars of dishes, fogged terrariums of glass.

 She foams a great white cloud of soap between her hands.

 She rubs them, runs the water, and forgets what she is doing.

 She strips down to her underwear, uncorks the wine.

 She pours a bright red ribbon in her glass.

 She sits and sips it.

•

Hello, mom.
 Yes, that's right.
 Black blouse. Gray skirt.
 Mhm.
 I don't know.
 I think, fine.
 I don't know.
 I said that I didn't know.
 I don't…
 I didn't mean…
 I didn't mean that I don't care.
 Yes, I do. I do, mom.
 Yes, of course I do.
 I'm sorry, mom.
 I didn't think of that.

•

She lies in bed and listens to the sounds of night, the rhythms of the highway, shuffled footsteps on the stairwell. She runs her right hand up and down her ribcage like a xylophone under her lifted nightgown, under shadow-fingered sheets.

 She plays her night game, which has slightly different rules:

Rule #1: Keep your eyes open.
Rule #2: Breathe slow, light breaths.
Rule #3: Lie on your side, facing the window.
Rule #4: Listen for all the different sounds outside the room.
Rule #5: Blend them together and convert them into words.
Rule #6: Blend them together and convert the words to phrases.
Rule #7: Repeat each phrase inside your head.
Rule #8: Do not respond with your own thoughts, or phrases.
Rule #9: Do not find any meaning in them.

The rhythms of the highway whisper, oh, hello, hello. The shuffled footsteps whisper oh, what, oh, what, why. The creaking movements of the floors above her whisper, hey, ah, hey. The radiator whispers, listen, listen, list.

•

Days pass.
　The curtains drift.
　The sounds paint shadows that she listens to.
　The bed sheets smell.
　The phone rings and she answers it.
　The water runs.
　The bath drain echoes.
　The pipes creak.
　The bed sheets sigh.
　The light stretches its tired hands across the floorboards.

•

She clicks her feet across the floor. She walks downstairs.
　She checks her mailbox. She has a new white envelope.
　She opens it.
　A new white letter slides into her hand.
　It reads:

I write to update you on the   Service Specialist  position.

I write to advise you that the hiring process is complete.

We interviewed a number of well-qualified job applicants. Ultimately, we decided on a more qualified applicant.

We hope you understand, and we sincerely thank you for your time. We wish you all the best in your endeavors.

•

    Hello, mom.
     Sorry. No, I haven't.
      No, I have. No, mom…I didn't.
       It's not…No…I can…No…I don't…
             mom, I…No, I…No…Please, don't say that, mom…
I…No, I…No, I…I try to be…But…No, I try…I try…But…
     Maybe…I'm just not that kind of person...mom…No…I know…
     I know, but…I know, mom, but, no, I know, but, mom, no…I know, but, mom, I know, but, MOM, NO, I SAID NO
                         NO
                 I
             SAID
        I
     SAID
  NO
 I'm still here…
Yes…No, mom…
I'm sorry…No…
    No…I won't…I'll…No…
   I'm so sorry…Yes…Ok. I will.
  I will. I will. I will. Don't worry.
  Mom. Don't worry. Oh. I'm so sorry. I will.

    Please, mom. Please, mom. I will. I will.
I'm sorry, mom.
I will.
I will.
I
love
you
too.

•

She hears the cars pass, distantly, a soft, consistent rhythm. She breathes through her nose. Her chest rises. It falls.
    She thinks about the ocean coming from a distance, through the phone. The expectation of its sound, which haunts all surfaces.
    She gets into remembered rhythms. She thinks, oh, what, oh, what, why, replays the sounds of rustling, the smells of different seasons.
    Upstairs, a vacuum starts. Of course, this interrupts the rhythm, starting with a rattled wheeze, then pacing back and forth in breathy whines.
    She thinks, it sounds like crying, like some lonely robot child.
    She thinks, that is me, somewhere inside.
    Some lonely robot child.

•

Meanwhile, hundreds of headlights form a shifting, shining pattern on the highway, beaming into falling snow, hundreds of thin, white lines that feel linked, their own bright streaming pathway, their own everlasting pathway, shifting, winding, separate from time.
    Somewhere beyond the highway, in the darkness, is a lake, a miniature ocean filled with vague, dark movements that the headlights cannot reach.
    But in a way, isn't the snow just falling bits of frozen lake?
    Bits of that dark expanse, turned small, to fall in sheets that disappear.

II

## SUGGESTIONS

You meet me in the field of corn behind the bunker hill. We both are playing war games and you tell me you are wounded. I always play the doctor since I am the only girl. I hold your arm and pinch your eyelids. I say, try to cry now.

You ask me for some clues for things to cry about. I make a few suggestions, like dead rabbits and divorce.

You picture a dirty old hare in your father's gray business suit.

You picture your father with knives in his chest and your mother with blood on her face.

# LOYALTY

The lake is a place to begin from, large enough to build your life around, as many families have tried to do. When looking on it from a distance, from the pine-draped hills, its shape is visible, a clear, distinctive S.

By day, the lake is just a mirror for the houses and the hills, the pebbled beaches, and a few small boats that slowly drift. The tall white mountain stands above the lake, beyond the hills, beyond the trees, beyond the reaches of the lake's reflection.

A house stands, separate from the rim of houses by the lake. The man inside it is a solitary man. He's built a chain link fence around his yard. A pair of large dogs paces around its perimeter.

The lake is a place to dwell in. Its clear shape fills empty sentences, begins, or—far more often—ends them with its cold, imagined depths. As night falls, outlines fade. The sky turns gray. The lake turns black. The tall white mountain stands, a shadowy suggestion.

A gentle mist gives way to thin, pale strips of fog, which rise into the trees, then hover there, like they are lost within them. The house stands, separate from the lake. The body of the man inside it lies dead on a mattress in the moonlight.

•

The dogs wander the backyard, scanning for their keeper, unsure why he hasn't come out from his house to fill their bowls. He has not done the things they see him do each day: Pour breakfast. Take them for a walk. Pour dinner. Take them for a walk.

Their coats are thick, gray layers over soft, white downy fur. They do not feel the chill of evening as the mist falls. They feel very hungry. They've already shared the last small bits of food left in their bowls, that morning, from the night before.

The younger dog, Orion, pokes his nose into his metal bowl. He scrapes his dish against the concrete slab of porch. His collar tags clink up against the metal of the bowl.

Scrape. Clink. Clink. Jingle. Scrape. Clink. Jingle. Jingle. Scrape.

The older dog, Artemis, looks around the yard. She finds a long forgotten toy, a rope that tastes like stale bread. She brings it to Orion. He licks at it, takes it in his mouth, and takes it to a corner of the fence.

Artemis walks onto the concrete porch slab and she sits. She looks at the glass sliding door, the long, white paneled blinds. She watches them to see if they are moving, or if they have moved, but they remain as still and white as bones.

•

Eight hundred miles away, inside a neighborhood, inside a home in Sacramento, all the kids are tucked in bed. A light, warm, late spring breeze drifts through the open windows, filling rooms with sweet, soft, airy, and unsettled feelings.

In the kitchen, the father sits, sipping iced tea at the counter. The mother stands, making a Memorial Day dinner. The father watches as the mother stirs and scoops, wraps things in cellophane, and shelves them in the fridge to serve tomorrow.

The mother scrapes a bowl of whipped up chocolate mousse into a pre-made pie shell, smoothes it gently with a spoon. She smoothes it carefully. She steps back and observes her work. She sighs. She scrapes the bowl again. She smoothes it out again.

What's that pie called? The father sips the last of his iced tea.

French Silk, the mother says.

It's French? he says.

She says, I don't know.

It is not my favorite pie, the father ventures, cautiously. He reconsiders. It's a bit of an odd pie. Unusual.

She says, it is, I guess, but it has always been his favorite.

He puts down his glass and he repeats, it is a bit of an odd pie.

The mother goes out of her way to make her brother's favorite things because he only visits once a year. She scrapes a bowl of whipped cream on the chocolate mousse, spooning and smoothing it with even greater care.

The father sees her lingering over this task. He recognizes a familiar tension in the muscles of her face. I've never been much of chocolate fan myself, he says.

She says, I'll make a coconut cream, too.

He says, now that's a pie.

•

Eight hundred miles away, the mist turns into rain. The dogs take shelter in their kennels, under plastic dome-shaped roofs. They slowly drift to sleep, still hungry, still unsure why they have not been fed, their ears pricked and tuned-in to every sound.

The rain taps gently at first, like soft, stroking fingertips. Then it taps harder, like the fingertips are scratching. Then it taps hard, like a whole hand beckoning toward its movement. The rain taps, come here, come here, come here, come here.

The dogs curl up deep into the shadows of their shelters, their own scent, which lines the shadows like a dark, thick sheet of breath. They watch the wet grass shiver in the rain until the moon shades and the shivers blur, and everything turns black.

•

It's 3 o'clock.

The father says, it's 3 o'clock.

She says, I know.

He says, well?

She says, well, I just don't know.

He sets the table with the plates, the cellophane-wrapped bowls. He reaches for the coconut cream pie. He almost reaches for the French Silk, but feels a tinge of sympathy. And anyway, he thinks, who needs French Silk?

He remembers a montage of past Memorial Day dinners with his girls, his wife, her brother and his pair of dogs. In each frame of his memory, his wife still makes the pie, still wears her blue-striped dress, her hair in tight-clipped nervous curls.

Each year, his wife retains this image even as his girls grow, bobbing through the yard, two yellow-headed sunflowers.

Her brothers' two small puppies have grown up as well, from friendly creatures playing in the yard, to larger adolescent dogs, kept leashed, to very large dogs hidden in their kennels in the basement. They're not used to kids, her brother always said when they would start to whine. The kids, the father always said to him, when he'd inevitably cut her brother off from drinking too much beer.

The father says, the kids are starving, and it's 3 o'clock.

The mother says, you go ahead. I'll wait a little while longer.

She stands by the front door, looking at the driveway, watching the curve around the bend, where she would just begin to see his car.

The father does the dishes.

Walks away. Comes back.

Dries off the dishes.

Walks away. Comes back.

Puts all the dishes in the cupboard.

Walks away. Comes back.

Looks at her.

You're still waiting?

She says, yes.

He says, the traffic, maybe.

She says, do you think I should call someone?

Of course, he does not tell her what he thinks.

She says, I think that I should call someone.

He gets the phone and gives it to his wife.

•

Orion and Artemis wake to the sound of a car pulling into the driveway. They rush to the edge of the gate. They look out through the links. The car looks different from their keeper's car. The man who opens the car door is not their keeper.

They hear some crackled noises coming from the man's hip pocket. Artemis growls into the direction of the sound. They hear a distant knocking. Pause. A knock. A voice. A knock. A voice. More crackled noises. More knocking. More crackled noises. Silence.

They hear a distant thud. An echo. Their ears flatten back. Orion barks, confused by the silence that follows as much as the sound.

The silence stretches on. Orion's ears resume their normal position, but Artemis still listens for the sound. She walks up to the sliding door. She watches for a movement in the blinds. A shadow shifts. A light darts back and forth inside.

•

The phone rings on the bedside table and the mother picks it up.
Hello?
Yes, this is she.
Oh. Yes. Oh. No. Oh. God.
Her eyes go wide. She looks straight forward, then she looks toward the father.
They—she hesitates—they found him in his house.
Of course, she says into the phone. Of course. No, not at all.
No, please, no, thank you, no, no, no, of course, no, no.
She holds the phone away from her.
The father takes the phone.
He says, hello, this is her husband.
I can do that.
Yes, I will. I will be there.
He rises from the bed. He tells the phone, one moment please.
He takes the mother's hand and holds it for a moment.
He walks into another room. No, I don't mind, he says.
Please don't apologize.
No, I should be the one.
He hears the mother through the wall, still crying to herself. He

hears the bed creak and the bed sheets rustling. He hears a muffled wail and a clenching sort of whine, like water trickling at a low pitch through the pipes.

He thinks, I should change my pitch to sound more thoughtful, less detached.

He says, it's easier for someone who is not related, yes.

He thinks, that didn't sound quite right. He thinks about what sounded wrong.

He says, someone who's not related, not by blood.

He thinks about blood, all the liquid flowing through a body.

He thinks about how this is going to be a fucking mess.

So much liquid.

So much flowing.

So much blood.

He thinks about the things a body holds inside, unseen.

He thinks a silent wave of wordless, tired, pissed off static.

In a softer voice, he says, out loud, I'm really not surprised.

•

The sun rises. A long car and a van pull up into the driveway. Neither is the shape or color of their keeper's car. Orion barks as three men step out and move toward the house. Artemis braces herself, letting out a low, deep growl.

They hear rustling and crackled noises like the night before. They see the mens' movements inside the house, behind the blinds. They see the men move up the stairs, lifting a long, flat plank. They hear soft bumping sounds. Orion barks. Artemis growls.

After awhile, they see the men move down the stairs, even more slowly, lifting up the flat plank with a long white sheeted form. They hear the door close, then, a harsh, metallic rattling. They see the men lift up the sheeted form into the van.

One of the men moves back to the house. He pulls the blinds back from the window. They can see him towering above them from behind the glass. Orion's ears fall flat. Artemis bares her teeth. The man jumps away from the window, pulls the blinds in place.

A moment later, the glass door slides open slightly, just a crack. A hand juts through the crack, sets down a bowl of water, slides it shut.

Another moment later, the door cracks again. A hand sets down another smaller bowl beside the bowl of water.

•

The father calls the office in the morning after emailing the form. He checks the empty box that says *bereavement*. He is careful to adjust his voice when speaking, so it sounds a little quivery, like maybe he is holding something back.

The HR Manager asks about his girls, the Six and Ten year-old, as he refers to them in office conversation.

He says, they are both good kids, but don't tell them I told you that.

Haha. Ok, the HR Manager replies.

The mother hasn't changed out of her nightgown. She's still on the couch, surrounded by her stacks of photo albums. He glances at her lap and and sees a page of Kodachromes: she and her brother, side-by-side, in matching sweaters.

It was so long ago, she says, as though she doesn't quite believe herself.

He doesn't know how to respond, so he says, yes.

It's how I think of him, she says. How I remember him.

He says, I think it's good of you to think of him that way.

Upstairs, Six and Ten stand in full dress at the sink. Their long blonde hair is pulled up into fuzzy yellow rubber bands. They both take their respective brushes—6 is pink and 10 is purple—and prepare them with their strips of blue mint paste.

He stands behind the doorway, watching their blue foaming mouths, their busy little movements, and he thinks, they really are good kids.

He says, be good, kids.

Ten spits and she says, we will, Dad.

Six spits and she smiles, flecks of toothpaste sticking to her teeth.

They eat the food inside their bowls.

They still feel hungry.

They pace around the yard.

They peer between the chain links of the fence.

No cars. No people. No new sounds or movements.

No colors, shapes, or smells signal the presence of their keeper.

Orion hunches on his elbows with his tail in the air. Artemis humors him and chases him around the yard. They tire of this quickly, and Orion takes his stale rope, lies down, and chews it by his corner of the fence.

Meanwhile, Artemis keeps pacing the perimeter. At first, she looks through all the openings, observes the lack of change, but as the day grows brighter, warmer, bringing no new sounds or movements, she moves faster, and the walls fade into blurs of light.

·

He cannot help but feel a sense of satisfaction as the city fades behind him, as his car becomes part of the highway's forward movement, a part of this shining current filled with metal bodies, filled with people, yet, entirely alone.

This is a feeling that he cherishes, a feeling that is typically confined to 10 weekly time slots from 8-9 and 5-6. When traffic halts, he glances at his fold-out map, the long blue vein of highway, flowing upward, flowing north.

The tall gray towers with their large white letters dwindle into short gray blocks of buildings, smaller roads, and smaller signs with smaller promises of places to refuel, places to rest, places where food can be purchased quickly, inexpensively.

As traffic thins, his stomach growls. He feels very hungry. He cannot remember the last time he felt so hungry. He pulls into a drive-through and he orders something that he never orders, something his wife would never let him eat.

He pulls back out onto the highway and drives onward, north. The gray blocks dwindle into sparse, gray houses, rise up into hills of trees. The houses grow fewer and fewer as the trees grow thicker. He peels back the crinkled wrapper, bites down into hot, bland meat.

He drives awhile, chewing, thinking, yes, it's good to be alone. It's good that I am getting something out of this.

He sees a dark, broad-winged bird, drifting gracefully above the trees.

He thinks, an eagle.

He looks closer. No, it is a vulture.

He drives past a group of vultures, drifting, all with equal elegance.

He thinks, I never knew that vultures were so beautiful.

He thinks, I'm only thinking that because the eagles aren't around.

He thinks, haha. Don't worry, eagles. I won't tell them.

He crumples up his fast food wrapper and he thinks about the eagles and the vultures and the beauty of the world.

He pulls around a curve and he's surrounded by great, bluish mountains, filled with darker bluish shadows from the clouds.

The shadows sweep across their smooth slopes in a feathered way, like the reflected strokes of many distant wings.

He passes by a mound of meat, a tarry mess of broken bones and blood and splattered organs.

He tries to think, just road kill, like he normally would think, but in these blue majestic shadows, normal thinking is impossible.

He thinks, a bird. He thinks, a car. He thinks, a person, driving.

He looks at his fast-food wrapper and feels guilty.

•

The flame pink sky burns down to cinder blue, then black.

The dogs sit side-by-side beneath the stars.

The grass grows cool, then damp.

The crickets chirp.

Waiting—waiting—waiting

An owl calls.

Who who—who who—who who

Eventually, they tire of watching for new movements, listening for new sounds, waiting for something to happen. They drift to sleep inside their igloo shelters, comforting themselves with fading traces of familiar smells.

Artemis dreams of running through some endless, mystic hills, just running, through green slopes, gold valleys filled with silver springs.

•

He stops for the night at a motel in the mountains. His room smells like stale smoke and old wood paneling. He stands inside a dingy plastic capsule underneath a moaning pipe, a rust-tinged trickling of water.

He towels off and lies, still damp, on top of all the sheets, closes his eyes, and thinks about his family at home. He thinks about his wife wearing her sweatshirt, with her hair pulled back, beneath the covers, reading from a story to the kids.

He thinks about Six and Ten, nodding off against her shoulders. Ten, in her purple nightgown. Six, in her pink nightgown.

He thinks about himself, sitting across from them, or, far more often, listening in on their voices from his chair downstairs.

He thinks about their low, hushed murmuring.

He thinks about his wife in bed, her low, hushed tears, her muffled whine.

He thinks of Six and Ten with their covers tucked up to their chins, their sleeping faces hidden underneath their hair.

He thinks about her brother's dogs. He wonders what they're doing and he tries hard not to think about that sound.

That awful crying from the basement.

Whimpers buried into whispers.

Into little quakes that rise up through the floors into his head.

•

They wait for the sound of the door, sliding open.

They wait to see the outline of their keeper in its entrance.

They wait for sounds of footsteps, scraping, shuffling around.

The sounds of rustled paper.

Tall gray stacks and towering black piles.

All the sour smells that come from them, within them, and around them.

Sour fluids pooling out across the floor.

•

He drives along a road surrounding a blue, serpentine lake, curving out from—then into—green forest hills. As he curves out from them, again, he sees the white slopes of the mountain, rising up through clouds like curling strands of steam.

The house sits just beyond the homes around the lake. To reach it, he must pull up through a long, deep shaded gravel drive. At the end of the drive sits a small, white paneled ranch home, set within a frame of tall, dark pines and long, lush plumes of fern.

His heart beats sharpen with the crackled sound the tires make as he pulls to the driveway's end and slows down to a stop. The wood around the single-car garage looks rotted. The house's roof is covered in crude patches, which are sagging in.

The dogs begin to bark as soon as he opens the car door. He takes a bag of food out of the trunk. Their barking deepens into growls as he comes closer to the gate, holding the bag up like a shield against his chest.

The dogs are poised behind the gate, backs arched, skin snarled up around their bright, pink gums, black lines of lips, their sharp, white teeth.

He murmurs, hey, dogs, hey.

He cracks the gate. The dogs continue growling.

He says, Artemis, Orion, in a firmer voice.

Orion's ears perk at his name, but Artemis waits til the gate is opened, til she sees his face, to soften.

He nods with great relief when they stop growling.

Hey, dogs. Hey.

He shifts his body through the gate in the order of its most replaceable parts.

They walk along with him, sniffing the bag of food. They lunge into the bowls, eating almost as fast as he can pour.

Good dogs, good dogs, he says.

He folds the empty bag beneath his arm. He watches, cautiously, to see what they will do.

Orion licks his mouth, then slowly creeps toward him, sniffs his hand, and looks up at the father with his warm, brown eyes.

•

Orion's old enough that he recalls a man who looks, and sounds, and smells just like this man. Yet, he is young enough that he also forgets things, easily. He trusts most men. He trusts the moment, as it comes. Artemis has a more developed sense of history, of loyalty—toward their keeper—mistrust—toward men.

•

He'd planned to spend the first day looking through the house, through his belongings, to see if there was anything of value he could save. He quickly learns that anything that was of value—once—has been so long neglected, it is no longer of use.

In the garage, he finds a once red car, now brown, a crust of dirt and withered leaves. When he approaches it, he hears an ominous, low hum. He peers in through the glass and sees a round, gray nest of hornets. He decides, there's nothing I can save in the garage.

He steps onto the porch. An indescribably bad smell drifts from the house. When he opens the door, it overwhelms him. He fishes through his pocket for the paper mask.

The entrance hall is filled with more tall stacks of cardboard boxes, carved into a shaky, narrow walkthrough. The hall becomes a larger space, no easier to move within, filled with neck-high piles of leaking garbage bags.

The walls: cracked, bleeding with tea-colored stains.

The ceiling: filled with brown and yellow blemishes.

Sick bubbles, burst.

Black mounds.

Accumulations, wept into a sort of skin.

Long, peeled strands that shimmer with the wings of flies.

•

The man fulfills the duties of their keeper, pouring food and water, calling for the dogs, calling their names. He offers them crisp braided biscuits when they come to him. They let him place new collars—blue and pink—around their necks. He never touches them, except to place the collars on, or clasp them to the edges of a leash.

His voice is soft, but he stands, stiffly, and he shifts from side to side.

His grip around the leash is very tight.

The man walks with the dogs, down the hill, down through the trees, until they reach the winding path that leads around the edges of the lake. He walks with them, past pebbled beaches, past the houses shadowed in the trees, past hundreds of bright, golden, blinking eyes.

•

He fills three dumpsters with the garbage from the house. As he begins to clear the surfaces, the smell grows even stronger.

The smell comes from a thick, black sludge. It's in the kitchen sink, the bathroom sink, the bath tub, and, of course, the toilet.

He smoothes a mound of vapor rub into his palm. He paints the skin around his nose with its protective glaze.

He scoops the thick, black, sludge out into buckets. He carries it out from the house, one bucket at a time.

He fills a garbage bag with beer cans that he finds, crushed in a sharp, metallic barricade around a bare, blue mattress.

He thinks, how can a person live like this?

He thinks, how *does* a person live like this?

Then, he remembers how this man would crush his beer cans at their table, sweep them to the side, and just continue eating.

He would look down, then, at his own, half-finished can, and feel strange, and feel guilty, as though he had done something.

He recalls thinking, I should say something to stop him.

But, from doing what? From being rude? From just behaving strangely?

His wife would come by, then, as though on cue, as though she knew his thoughts, reach out and wordlessly take all the cans away.

•

The sky turns pink.

The man calls out their names.

Orion trots up to him as he pulls the biscuit from the bag.

He nuzzles up against his hand. The man stays stiff, at first, but when Orion's finished eating, he puts out his hand. He strokes his head.

Artemis joins them, and she nuzzles up against the man. He strokes around her mane and she moves closer to his side. For just a moment, though, she loses track of where his hand has gone. She makes a deep sound he interprets as a warning.

He puts the collars on their necks. He clasps the leashes. They move together down the hills, toward the lake. He doesn't seem to move as stiffly, now. He doesn't hold their leashes quite as tightly in his hands.

The crickets chirp. Orion sniffs a small, thin tree. A spider spins a dewy little web within its branches. Another man and a young girl are walking toward them, just a set of distant human shapes that barely register.

Beneath the water, strands of yellow grass twitch from a darting fish. A light breeze makes the long reeds quiver on the lake. The flame pink of the sky burns bright against the mountain and its mist of clouds, the colors of some strange emergency.

Suddenly, the girl breaks from the man. She runs with hands outstretched toward the dogs. She shouts out, small and fast and loud. The young girl and her smallness and her fastness and her loudness frighten them. As she runs near to them, the dogs begin to growl.

She reaches out a clumsy hand toward Artemis, who arches defensively, then snaps into the air.

The distant man shouts and the young girl runs toward him, crying.

The man they know pulls back the walking strings so hard they cannot breathe.

•

From his hotel, the father calls a purebred rescue center. A woman answers with a warm and calming voice. He asks her if someone can come to take the dogs. He tells her they are beautiful and very well-behaved.

She asks their breed, their age. She winces when the father tells her. She apologizes, but she says she cannot take them. If they were younger, it might be a possibility, perhaps. But not that breed, and not that age. They won't adapt to a new family.

The father says, I think that there might be a chance. They're good and they're so loyal. They are very loyal dogs.

But sadly, that is just the problem, she explains. The dogs are loyal to the lives that they have always known.

She offers to contact an animal technician who will come to pick them up, to put the dogs to sleep. She says, I'm sorry, once again. She really means it. They will be there by tomorrow morning, she says. Free of charge.

He hangs up.

Shuts his eyes.

His chest is filled with that familiar sadness that he felt, hearing the dogs, their whimpers rising from the basement.

He tells himself this sadness is the same, strange guilt he felt whenever he would watch his wife come take her brother's cans.

He tells himself he's doing nothing wrong.

He's doing nothing wrong.

It's not his house and they are not his dogs.

He's doing the right thing for them.
The woman on the phone agreed.
He thinks, her voice was warm and calm.
She sounded very kind.

•

Orion and Artemis drift to sleep inside their shelters, dreaming ordinary dreams of running, playing, grass, and trees, and lakes.
The grass is soft.
The trees are tall.
The lake is wet.
The air is crisp.
Their lives are what they are.
And they are what they are within them.

•

When he arrives that morning, he waits for the animal technician's van to pull up in the gravel drive behind him.
He walks through the gate.
He pours their food as usual.
He pets Artemis behind her ears.
He pats Orion gently on his head.
He leashes them. He leads them out onto the driveway, where the animal technician waits to lead them to the van.
He does not watch as they are led into the van.
He does not watch the van as it backs down the driveway, then pulls out and drives away.
He walks around the house, now empty, with its filthy, mold-encrusted carpet, yellow, brown, and black stains on the walls.
He stares into the stains.
Imagines islands on a map.
Small, stony bodies.
Shapes emerging from the darkness of a lake.

# WHITE SCARS

She has a broad scar that runs over the back of her kneecap. The skin is all shiny and soft, like white bread packaged in Saran Wrap.

I kiss it, ask her how it happened, and she mumbles, face pressed down into the pillow where she has been sleeping.

A month or so later, who knows, I am kissing a man in that position. I look for a shiny white scar on the back of his knee. I feel strange when it isn't there, like I have willed an injury. My memory has punished him for being someone else.

I kiss the soft skin where there is no scar.

I look up at the peeling paint along the ceiling.

I smile at the ceiling. I say, look at that. You're healed.

He turns his head, pretending that he doesn't hear me.

# INVENTORY

The Night Staff is responsible for inventory. Each shift, first thing, he reaches for his binder filled with lists. These lists are items he must organize, clean, and prepare. These lists are tasks that he must check in boxes.

There is a list for each room in this house. It's called a group home. It is not much of a home. It is a long rectangle hall, white walled on both the outside and the inside. He moves down the hall. He sorts through shelves of labeled boxes, bottles, lists.

The Night Staff checks the boxes for the kitchen. Dishes, counters, fridge cleaned. Cabinets stocked. Sharps, tubes, pill grinders sterilized. He checks the boxes for the bathrooms. Bathtubs, counters, floors, and toilets cleaned. The medication count, checked by the Day Staff before him.

He checks the laundry room. He checks detergents, sprays, and soaps. How many they have and how many more they need. He puts the laundry in. He takes it out. He folds it, separating clothing into piles labeled with each resident's initials.

The clothing, even when clean, smells of urine.

The hall, the rooms, though clean, all smell of urine.

The Night Staff checks each bedroom to make sure the residents are sleeping. He removes his gloves and turns each handle slowly. He cracks just enough space to peer into the rooms. He sees still, sleeping bodies, skinny faces, open mouthed.

He listens for their breathing. Gentle hissing, quiet hums. Low, crackled murmurs. Shadowed limbs locked into long, white bars of moonlight.

He closes each door, quietly, checks boxes for each resident. 9pm. 10pm. 11pm. 12pm.

When all the lists are checked, the Night Staff walks back down the hall, sits down, and sinks into a soft blue haze of television.

The clock ticks through the blue glow. It is 5am. His body feels like it's filled with thick, half-frozen fluid. The fluorescent hall light flutters, casting pale, half shadows on the floor. The shadows move like ghostly fingers flicking something off their hands.

A door clicks. Then, it creaks. The Night Staff tilts his head. He waits. He hears the sound of slippers scraping down the hall.

He whispers, hey, JB.

JB coughs lightly and continues scraping forward, flannel print pajamas soaked and sticking to his legs.

Looks like you had an accident, he says.

JB nods. Sorry.

It's okay, he says. Come on. I'll help you get cleaned up.

He grabs a binder and a plastic box and a set of fresh-laundered clothes, all labeled with the letters: JB.

Inside the bathroom, JB takes his dirty clothes off, puts them in the hamper, then stands naked with his arms outstretched. JB looks out the bathroom window, which is blocked off by metal bars that the Night Staff installed the last time that he broke it.

The Night Staff opens up the binder to an unmarked diagram, the outlines of two sexless, faceless bodies. The bodies in these diagrams appear to hover strangely, like life forms floating downward in a cold white beam.

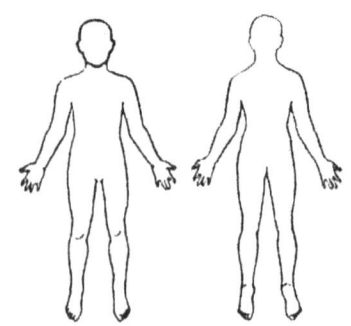

The Night Staff scans JB for new scars, bruises, bites, and injuries, makes note of them within the diagram. The sexless, faceless forms accumulate small markings: scribbled words and arrows drawn to slashes, spots, and shades.

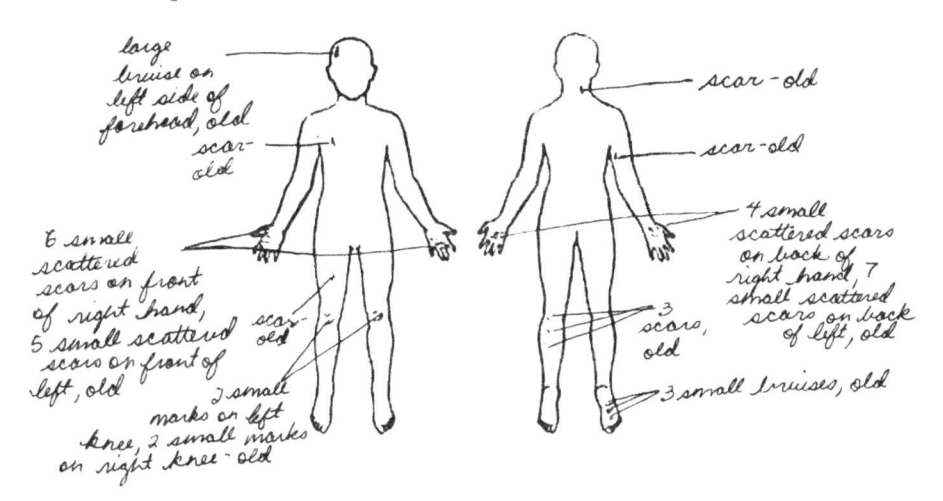

*large bruise on left side of forehead, old*
*scar - old*
*scar - old*
*scar - old*
*6 small scattered scars on front of right hand, 5 small scattered scars on front of left, old*
*scar - old*
*4 small scattered scars on back of right hand, 7 small scattered scars on back of left, old*
*3 scars, old*
*3 small bruises, old*
*2 small marks on left knee, 2 small marks on right knee - old*

He always draws an X beside new markings. All of JB's marks are old, though. Self-inflicted wounds.

The indentations on his legs: from JB's teeth, the mornings when he sits, legs folded to his chest, and nibbles at his knees.

The bruise on his forehead: from the afternoon last week when JB wailed, suddenly, and slammed his head into the wall.

The scars along his hands: from the last time he broke the window in the bathroom, when he hurled himself out into the street.

The scabs and bruises on the bottoms of his feet: from bits of broken glass and gravel he picked up while running.

Other scattered scars: from JB's mother, from before he lived here, from before they came to take JB away.

JB stands, naked skin accumulating goosebumps, bleeding, picked, or nibbled scabs, white edged and soggy, steeped in piss. He shivers.

We're almost finished, bud, the Night Staff says.

JB stares out the window.

The Night Staff closes the binder and he clicks his pen.

•

It is 6am. JB sits, cleaned and dressed, beside the Night Staff on the couch. He shifts and rocks. His legs are folded to his chest. He mutters to himself. The Night Staff whispers, quiet. JB's mutter softens to a murmur, than a low-pitched hum.

•

The Day Staff arrives at 7am. He nods and the Night Staff nods.
JB is rocking back and forth and mumbling.
Oh gimme dat fuck dat sweet datass. Oh gimme dat fuck dat sweet datass. Oh gimme dat fuck dat sweet datass, he mumbles.
The Day Staff smirks. Aint nothin wrong with JB.
The Night Staff heads out to the back porch with the Day Staff. They smoke a cigarette. This helps him redirect his thoughts. That is the term they use, when writing incident reports. The residents act out and they redirect the residents' behavior.
They sit across from one another on two rusted metal chairs. The yard is dry, brown grass surrounded by a chain-link fence. There is a light frost. There's a mourning dove perched on the piled remnants of an old tree house that no one ever used.
The sunlight is beginning to ignite the fringes of the sky, which still remains this cold, flat, yellow gray. The Night Staff looks out at the sky. He tries to focus on the curling strands of smoke. There's something in this yellowed sky that terrifies him.
That JB, says the Day Staff.
The Night Staff says, I know.
I think he gets it, says the Day Staff.
The Night Staff says, more than we know.
The Day Staff just shakes his head. He says, sometimes I think about it. Fuck. If I were him, I'd kill myself.

•

At 7:15am, the Night Staff's girlfriend comes to take him home.
She texts his phone. The text says: I'm outside.
He texts her back: okay.
He walks back down the hall, one last time. All the residents are starting to wake up. Meanwhile, JB vaults his body back and forth into a giant reddish callisthenic bouncy ball.
Oh gimme dat fuck dat sweet datass, datass, datass, datass, says JB.
The Day Staff looks over at him, bouncing back and forth. He shakes his head. Nope, there aint nothin wrong with JB.

•

His girlfriend leans to kiss him when he gets into the car. He slumps into the seat. It looks like he's avoiding her. She says, how was your night, but it does not come out like she's asking a question. He ignores it. Or he doesn't really hear her.
The skinny, leafless trees, the light gray houses and retention ponds, the flocks of geese, the curling outlets into dark inlets of woods, the strip malls, curving, pillared highways, underpassing, overpassing, rolling by the fog-glazed window on some sad conveyer belt.
She's talking about something she was doing last night with someone she knows, someone she's known for quite awhile, though he can't remember how she knows this person and he's never met this person and he can't remember what she does because he doesn't care.
As she pulls into the gravel back lot of their small, plain duplex, she leans over, once again, and tries to kiss him.
He looks back at her.
She's giving him a strange look.
He says, what.
She says, nothing.
He says, okay, then, and he goes inside the house.
They look at the clock. It is 7:52am. Gotta run, says his girlfriend.
Okay, he says. Hope work goes well.
She says, thanks. See you later, she mutters, I guess, but the door shuts the sound of her sentence.

He pulls a blanket off the couch. He shuffles to the kitchen, gets a mug. He gets a fifth of Evan Williams. He fills the mug up to the brim and sips it gingerly. He shuffles to the couch, sinks down, and switches on the television.

•

Hey. Hey. He sees his girlfriend as a dark blur, leaning over him.

He squints. What time is it?

She says, it's almost 5pm.

Off in the background, the television is a coldly buzzing bluish ocean filled with aimless waves of endless conversation.

What's it like, outside? he asks.

It's snowing, she says.

Oh, he says.

He thinks about the snow, the cold, his memories of cold and snow. He thinks of his childhood, like everyone else, when they think of the snow. He feels a deep pang start to trickle through his chest.

She kisses him. He kisses her. She sits down on the couch. He sits up. She leans in. He leans in. She pulls back the blanket. He pulls back her hair. He pushes up her sweater. She pushes her mouth into his mouth, her body closer to his body.

Her mouth tastes like cigarettes, cheap bread, and peanut butter. He keeps kissing, knowing his mouth tastes like sour sleep and Evan Williams. Her hair smells like cigarettes and stale perfume. He keeps touching her, knowing he smells like bulk antiseptic and wet vinyl gloves.

He gets it up and she gets on it for a little while.

On the television, a chef with a kind, round face stirs a bubbling white sauce.

Mm-mm. The chef sips at the sauce.

Mm-mm. His girlfriend lightly moans.

He holds her tighter and looks at her head so he won't see the screen. He focuses in on the bright blue rubber band that holds her hair. He thinks about the rubber gloves he wears to clean at work. The band bobs up and down and up and down and up and down.

This sauce was handed down to me by my mother, the television chef says, and her mother, and her mother, and her mother before her.

His girlfriend digs her nails deep into his skin.

He thinks, that's nice.

It tastes like family, the chef declares.

It tastes like love.

•

She brews a pot of coffee and she sets their cups down, gravely.

Look, we have to talk, she says.

He says, okay.

They sit together, silently, drinking their coffee for a moment.

They look out the kitchen window at the snow.

She starts to tell him about someone she is meeting somewhere. Someone that he doesn't know. She says, I love you, but…

He is not listening.

He's thinking about love.

He's thinking about family.

He's thinking of the snowmen he has built throughout his life.

He pictures them all lined up, staring at him through the window with their weird misshapen heads, their clumsy faces framed in twigs.

He hears his girlfriend saying, - - - - - - - - It's not that I don't love you - - - - I love you, but I'm - - - - - - sorry, baby - - - - - but, you know. I'm tired.

He looks out at the snowmen looking at him with their vacant eyes. Some filled with charcoal, some with stones, some left unfilled.

He thinks, what are you doing here? I thought that you were gone.

All of the snowmen slowly shake their heads in unison.

•

She drops him off at work at 8:02pm. The sky is black. The snow keeps coming down. The windshield wipers sweep them into arches. In the lamplight, they look like a pair of newly opened eyes watching the snow, which moves like swarms of shining insects.

He says, I'll see you soon.

She mutters something.

He says, drive home carefully. The snow.

She says she will. She drives away.

He watches as the snow begins to fill her tire tracks. He watches as her taillights fade into darkness.

•

Tonight, the house is filled with a bad energy. The Day Staff stays late to mitigate the rising chaos. The residents are fighting. One attempts to break a chair. Another breaks the glass case for the fire extinguisher.

Another kid shits in the bathtub. After cleaning up, the Day Staff (a new hire) cracks the window to air out the room. While the Day Staff breaks up the fight, JB breaks through the window. He triggers the motion sensor, which sets off the house alarm.

The Night Staff chases JB through the side yard, through the front yard, down the sidewalk, down the road that leads out to the highway. Thick, white clouds of heavy breathing trail past them. JB's bare feet leave long, flat tracks, like a rabbit running through the snow. JB slips on a patch of ice. The Night Staff catches up. He wraps his arms around him. This is called a basket hold. It's what they're trained to do. He crouches down over JB, both of them panting, eyes wide. He holds firmly. He says, JB, no. You need to stay here.

The Night Staff feels JB's shoulders, wet and heaving.

JB twists a little in his hold. He mumbles, why?

The Night Staff grips him tighter. He says, this is where you live.

JB stops twisting. He takes a deep breath.

The Night Staff loosens up his grip, a bit.

He says, it's cold. We should go back inside.

JB says, sorry.

The Night Staff says, do you understand?

JB says, chocolate milk.

The Night Staff thinks, I think he means hot chocolate.
JB repeats, chocolate milk.
The Night Staff thinks, that is a good idea.
He says, do you understand?
JB grumbles and shifts around.
He pulls JB to his feet. They stand up together.
He just keeps repeating, do you understand, do you understand?
JB keeps repeating, chocolate milk, chocolate milk.

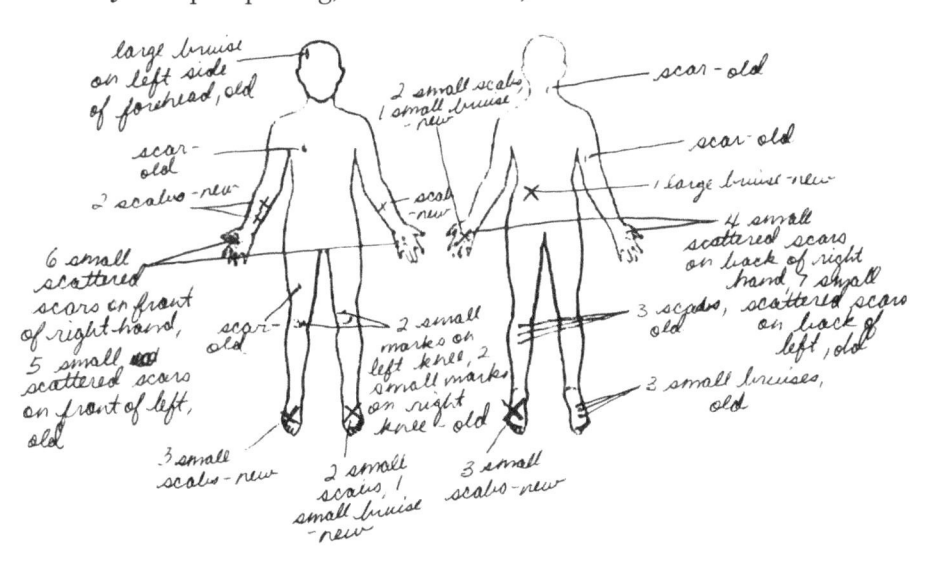

*[Diagram of front and back views of a body with handwritten annotations:
- large bruise on left side of forehead, old
- scar - old
- 2 scabs - new
- 6 small scattered scars on front of right hand, 5 small scattered scars on front of left, old
- scar - old
- 3 small scabs - new
- 2 small scabs, 1 small bruise - new
- 2 small marks on left knee, 2 small marks on right knee - old
- 3 small scabs - new
- 2 small scabs, 1 small bruise - new
- scar - old
- scab - new
- scar - old
- scar - old
- large bruise - new
- 4 small scattered scars on back of right hand, 7 small scattered scars on back of left, old
- 3 scabs - old
- 2 small bruises, old]*

•

His girlfriend texts him at 11:32pm.
    The text says: You should find another ride.
    He texts her back: What's up? Why are you going to be late?
    She texts him back: I'm sorry. You should find another ride.
    He calls her phone. The call goes straight to voicemail. He thinks, shit.
    He texts her back: Why are you going to be late?
    He calls her phone again. The call goes straight to voicemail.
    He texts her back: Where are you?
    He sits and thinks about where she might be.

•

The Night Staff cleans each room and he takes inventory. He flips through his binder, checks all of his lists. He checks on all the residents, all fast asleep, thin faces quivering. 12am. 1am. 2am. 3am.

He makes a cup of instant coffee and a cold cheese sandwich. He stands in the kitchen, watching the light flickering. The urine smell still lingers, so he eats as fast as possible. He tastes the urine smell in each bite as he eats.

On the television, a heavily tattooed man is speaking from some prison on MSNBC: Lockup.

He says, it gets hard, but my baby just keeps sending letters.

I write, baby, just keep sending me your letters.

I need to hear from her, to know that she remembers me.

I tell her, I don't care what you say, just keep sending me your letters.

He makes another cup of coffee and he gulps it down. He checks his phone. It's 3:13am and he has no new messages. He watches the light flickering. He checks his phone. It's 3:15am and he has no new messages. He thinks, shit. He walks down the hall. He walks back. He checks his phone. It's 3:18am and he has no new messages. He slumps into the chair. He watches prisoners explain how they communicate. He watches them explain how they make shanks. He feels a sharpness in his gut. He checks his phone. It's 3:30am and he has no new messages.

•

The Day Staff arrives at 7am. They nod and the Night Staff nods.

He goes to the back porch to smoke a cigarette.

The Day Staff says, how's it going?

The Night Staff says, I don't know.

They sit in silence.

The Night Staff scrolls through his texts.

•

It is 7:15am and he has no new messages. It is 7:15am and she has not arrived.

He zips his coat and pulls the hood around his face. It's almost three miles walking distance from the group home to his home.

The branches of the trees hang low, like crystal skeletons. The sky is that sad yellow gray that terrifies him. He passes a flat, frozen pond. The pond reflects the equally flat faces of the houses that surround it.

He takes a shortcut through the neighborhood. He passes snow forts and snow angels, human outlines in the ground. He sees a snow man. He approaches it. He looks into its hollowed eyes. They look back at him. He thinks, fuck you.

The wind blows back his hood when he crosses the highway bridge. His face is numb with cold. His eyes are filled with lukewarm tears. He wipes them with his gloved hand, where they chill to nubs of frost. The sun is peeking through the clouds, shining its yellow gray pathetic light.

•

When he gets home, her car isn't parked in the back. He walks a few blocks back and forth. She is not parked along the street. He walks around the neighborhood. He circles round, then back a few times to the space he knows she should be parked in.

She is not inside the house. He thinks, maybe she had to work. He thinks, yeah. Then he thinks, no. Then, he thinks, I will not think about it.

He grabs for his blanket, shuffles to the kitchen. Suddenly, he's hungry. He flips through the cabinets and grabs a box of noodles. He thinks, chocolate milk. He makes a sound that wants to be a laugh. He grabs a dusty packet of powdered hot cocoa.

He pours water for the noodles and the cocoa, nukes the cocoa in the microwave, and stands there, staring at the stove's blue flame.

He pours a splash of Evan Williams in the cocoa. Takes a sip. He adds another splash. He sips. He adds another.

He thinks, yeah, I'll bet she had to work. He thinks, no. He thinks, chocolate milk, chocolate milk. He drinks his cocoa.

He checks his phone. It's 9:27am and he has no new messages. He eats his noodles, finishes his cocoa. He checks his phone. It's 9:38am and he has no new messages. He walks to the couch, sits down. He checks his phone. It's 9:40am and he has no new messages.

He calls. No answer. Puts the phone back down. Gets up. Puts dishes in the sink. Picks up the phone. Puts it back down, then picks it up.

He calls. No answer. He listens to her voicemail message. Her voice stops speaking. Beep. He listens to his silence.

He shuffles to his bedroom. He opens the closet. Hangers pushed to his side. Half the closet is now empty.

He watches himself playing with the hangers in the closet mirror. He watches himself lowering the blanket. He watches himself take his shirt off, then, his pants, then, all his clothes. He watches and he looks, but mostly waits.

He tries to picture what he used to look like, when they met. He can't remember. He cannot remember what she would have seen.

He stands there, looking, hoping that his body will reveal something. He stands, watching for himself, but all he sees is:

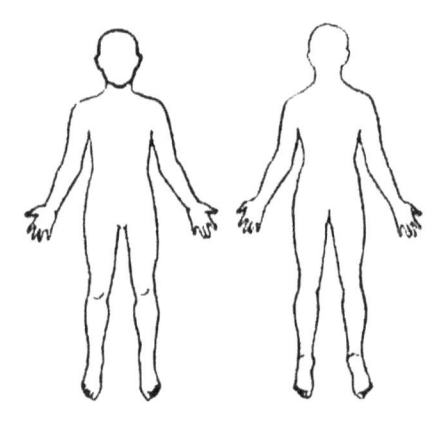

•

He wakes up where he passed out on the couch. He checks his phone. It is 5:03pm and he has no new messages. She'd usually be home by now, he thinks. She isn't coming home. He thinks, oh. Shit. I guess that means I have to leave for work.

He still feels foggy from the Evan Williams. And everything else. He makes a pot of coffee. Drinks a cup. Tastes shitty.

He brushes his teeth. Glances at the mirror. Looks down. Spits. He runs the faucet, then looks slowly back into the mirror. He thinks, I guess this is it. He drinks a sip of water, swishes it around his mouth. He swallows a cold stream of his saliva.

•

The group home, once again, is a chaotic atmosphere. JB is tearing back and forth across the hall. He's yelling out the lyrics of another song. He sings, I wanna get with you oh yeah I wanna get with you.

On one of these jaunts through the hall, JB runs out the back door. The alarms sound. The Night Staff runs after him across the yard. He catches him before he hits the fence. He says, remember, this is where you live.

JB whispers, I wanna get with you oh yeah.

The Night Staff leads JB back to the living room. JB looks him directly in the eye. JB makes a fist, four fingers curled, thumb pointed toward his face. He touches his thumb twice against his lip and waits expectantly.

The Night Staff says, I think he's signing private time.

The Day Staff rolls his eyes. No shit JB wants private time.

The Night Staff shrugs. He is a human being. He has needs.

The Day Staff groans. Monitor him, he says. Have him crack the door.

The Night Staff drags a chair in front of JB's bedroom door.

He says, it's okay, JB. You can go have private time. He winces. I need to sit by the door, he says. I need to watch you because you were running out. We don't want you to get hurt, so that's why I need to watch you.

JB stares back, wide eyed. He says, okay. He runs into his room. He flops back on the bed. The bedsprings shriek.

The Night Staff cracks the door just wide enough to hear JB. He hears the bed springs going creak, krrcreak, krrcreak. He stares into the door. He traces the wood grain. There are so many spots that look like eyes. He looks at them and feels like he's being watched.

•

The Night Staff cleans each room and takes inventory. He checks off his lists. He checks on all the residents. He paces back and forth across the hallway. He paces the laundry room. He paces back and forth across the kitchen.

He pours a couple saltine crackers in a bowl. The bowl is cheap, tan, and plastic covered with thin hairline cracks. He notices that there are teeth marks on one side. He contemplates throwing his crackers out. He puts one in his mouth. It tastes okay.

The Night Staff sinks into his chair. The television glows. His phone glows in his pocket. The hall light glows dimly.

He feels for his phone. He thinks, the Day Staff is wrong. I wouldn't kill myself.

He sits and watches, waiting for this night to end.

•

He calls his girlfriend and she doesn't answer. He thinks, should I leave a message? He thinks, I should think about it.

Then, he thinks about the vast accumulation of their days. These days unfurl, indistinguishably, in a band of gray.

The band gets wrapped around his thoughts and he cannot tell what he's thinking. He thinks, that is the way it's always been.

He thinks about the stale smell that lingers in their home, the way the yellow morning light illuminates the dust, the way the dust collects, the way it shimmers in the light, the way it rises, shining, shivering, obscuring everything.

He thinks about the dust. He thinks about the yellow gray.

He thinks, whatever she was thinking, she was right.

He nods back at the Day Staff when he arrives at 7am, but he doesn't join him for a cigarette. He has a long walk through the cold ahead of him.

He walks along the lines of frail trees and houses. The sky is still dark, in the beginning, just beginning to turn gray. He watches as the yellow halo of the highway lamps becomes the morning light, begins to disappear.

A flock of pigeons flies across the highway. He admires how their shadows move. They're like a banner of black stars. He pauses for a moment and he watches how their shadows move. He watches and tries to feel the things he should be feeling.

III

# SUNFLOWERS

I say haha, look at this. It's me when I was twelve. I am wearing a floppy red hat with a sunflower on it, in the picture.

I am wearing no hat, now.

My hair is black and straightened, now.

Not in the picture. In the picture it is brown.

It's mousey couch-like brown. And I am sitting on a couch. My dog is sitting on it, in it, next to me. She's dead now.

You tell me, damn, girl, you were ugly.

I smile, showing off my braces.

In the picture, I am smiling.

But not now.

I open my hand, and I close my hand, look at my hand, like I think it's a locket, there, right there, inside, I will open it up, and there, right there, inside of my hand, I will see myself.

A picture of the person that I still may be, somewhere in there.

Still smiling with my black hair, red hat, sunflowers.

# AFRAID OF THE RAIN

The light within the curtains is the first thing that she sees. A tired light. A meager shadowing of lattices. A light like skin stretched tight across an aching ribcage. She breathes in. She breathes out. Turns toward his indentation in the sheets.

She hears the water from behind the bathroom door. She shuts her eyes. She runs her hand across the empty sheets. Trickling and splashing. That sound that the pipes make when the water shuts off, like a heavy protestation. Dripping echoes down the drain.

Her husband creaks the door. She squints toward him. He is in his suit and tie. He sprays cologne. Light drifts of cedar wood, citrus, and vetiver.

She says, that one's my favorite.

He says, yes. I know it is.

He comes over beside the bed. He kneels with a gentle groaning sound.

He smoothes her hair. She says, how does it feel?

He breathes in. He breathes out.

He says, it feels good. Last time I wear this suit.

He kisses her forehead. He stands and adjusts his tie.

What time do you think you'll be home? She says.

He says, the usual.

She nods.

He smiles. Maybe just a little early. I'll bring brandy for the cake.

She yawns. That would be nice.

He puts his hand over her hand. He says, I love you. So much.

She says, I love you too.

He stands there for a moment, looking at her, putting his hands in his pockets, taking them back out. I'll see you soon, he says. He walks away and shuts the door. She watches as the narrow line of light diminishes until he closes it behind him.

She leans toward the window, listening as his car pulls out into the tired morning light. She swallows, thinking, see you soon. She holds her breath.

She hears a bird call to another bird. A distant echo. She can hear the pavement crackle, tires whining like they always do.

•

She lies there for what feels like a long time. She keeps listing all the things she needs to do. Everything on this list seems impossible. She feels so tired. She wonders how she has done these things for so long.

She needs to do the dishes
Make the coffee
Sort through all the mail
Pay the bills
Make envelopes for bills that have not come
Walk to the grocery store
Purchase the groceries
Walk the long way home, for once
Get home and mix the cake
Put the cake in the oven
Take the cake out at the right time, so it's almost finished when he gets home
Let it sit
Fill in the filling
Icing
Serve it in the blue green dish

She imagines the cake. The reddish layers must be perfect. Burgundy. The icing must be perfect white, with peaks like little waves. That's why she thinks that she should use the blue green serving dish. The way the waves of icing make the cake look like a painting of the ocean.

While she's thinking, she is staring at the ceiling, which is covered in this foam-like texture. She cannot remember what it's called. In her mind, as she lists each item on the list, she jumps from one splash of this foam-like textured ceiling to another.

Dishes
Coffee
Mail
Bills
Envelopes
Cake

Stuccoing. That is what it's called. Of course. Stuccoing. She remembers now.

Outside this room, her neighbors are enveloped in the day. The smell of burning leaves drifts through the curtains, which are filled with light.

•

She lines the dishes on the drying rack. It's like a metal skeleton with rows of white ceramic organs. The steam rises. She dries off her hands. The smell of burning leaves mingles with lemon. She stands over the sink, stares into the drain.

She grinds the coffee, pours it in the filter, pours the water in the tank, then waits and listens for that sacred churling sound.

Another wave of steam. She breathes in. She breathes out. She holds the coffee in both hands. She sips it like she's sipping from a golden chalice.

•

She hesitates when she enters the grocery store. Should she take the cart, or the basket? She contemplates the pros and cons. She doesn't need too much, but need feels complicated, now. She doesn't need a cake, after all, when you think of it that way.

The cart is a commitment, she thinks, but the basket's too small. She feels like she often takes the basket, then regrets it. She wheels out the cart. The wheels shriek. The cart is filled with scattered coupons, flattened and forgotten.

She gets the
~~Flour~~
~~Sugar~~
~~Baking soda~~
~~Vegetable oil~~
~~Vanilla extract~~

Cocoa. Here, she hesitates, again. She gets the most expensive. When she picks the milk, she also picks the most expensive.

As she's heading toward the checkout line, she passes through the aisle with the chocolate. She sees something that she likes. A little truffle, pocket-sized. Her heart beats faster and she slips it in her purse. She hasn't done this since she was a little girl.

When the groceries are rung up, she does not take her receipt. She does not want to see what she bought or what it cost. It is a challenge, but she knows there is no point to it, that way of thinking. Now. She must try. She does not want to see things that way.

•

She walks home the long way through the park. The air is filled with smoke. The burning leaves. The sounds of children on the swings. The creaking sounds, like sad, robotic birds. The chattering of leaves. The scraping of their small shoes, back and forth across the blacktop.

She thinks, John. She cuts away from them into the trees. The tall pines, drowning out their smoke, their sound, their drifting movements. She thinks, John. She thinks, don't think about it. She thinks, you decided, didn't you. You will not think of things like that, or in that way.

She reaches the lagoon. This is the reason she came through the park, to stand here on the wood bridge, look into the water. She looks at the willow branches, dipping down into the pond. The tree's reflection, gray-washed, quivering, and upside-down.

The branches bend in waves and trickles. Tiny star-shaped insects skate across the pond. A breeze. A deeper chill runs through her. A small flock of ducks swoops down and lands in scatters. Water splashing. Branches rustling. The sun comes out. She hears a couple laughing in the distance.

She walks through the park onto the overpass. The bars across the interstate create a cage of shadows. Now, her shadow crosses through the cage. She peers over the edge. She feels the rush of wind, the downward pull from each car as it passes.

•

She opens all the mail, reads it, pays the bills. She makes notes of the things she needs to put inside the other envelopes. She folds the stubs of all the bills, arranges them inside one of the envelopes. She's keeping them inside a set of files in the kitchen drawer.

The wheel runners of the drawer make a rolling sound. The drawer makes a small, stiff clicking when it closes. Then, a silence. She sits at the table and unwraps her chocolate. Gold foil crinkles at her fingertips. The truffle in her mouth.

She breathes in. She can taste an undertone of wine-like berries. Not bad. It reminds her of something she cannot trace. She thinks, John, then.

She wants to call him. She looks toward the phone. She doesn't call him. She swallows her chocolate, folds the crinkled wrapper. Now is not the time.

•

She turns the dial to pre-heat the oven. Click. She hears a warm reverberation, a soft, hollow rattling. She rubs a buttered pad around the edges of the pan. She dusts with flour. She whisks dry ingredients in one bowl, pours the milk into another. She drips drops of red into the milk. Before she stirs, she watches them dissolve, each separate, ghostly disappearance.

She sits down and she looks up at the clock, a circle in the middle of a set of slim, sleek silver rays. She thinks, it's probably worth money, now. She watches the hand make its revolution. Strange, to think about these things being worth money.

Now, the time is right, so she takes out the timer. Click. She slides the metal rounds into the oven and she waits. The ticking of the timer fills the room.

She rubs her temples. Click click click click click click click click click.

The warm, sweet smell. The curtains drifting in the fading light.

•

He comes home bearing bags of food bought from the deli, plastic tubs of pasta, three bean salad, and rosemary roasted vegetables, two sandwiches in crinkly brown paper, and, as promised, a new bottle of her favorite brandy. He sets a bag of fried mushrooms and cauliflower on the counter. Pestos, marinara, and a jar of flavored olives.

It's like Christmas morning, she says, opening the olives, fingering around the sprigs of lavender and lemon peel.

That's what I hoped for, he smiles. He makes both their plates. They sit together, chewing quietly, with small, pleased murmurs.

She dabs at her mouth. It's more than we can eat.

He sighs. I know.

They sit there, silently. She looks down at the oils gathered on her plate.

She runs a finger through them, bursting bubbles into smaller bubbles into smaller, smaller, smaller bubbles.

•

She returns to the cake rounds, which have cooled, runs a knife around the rims of both the pans, shivers them back and forth. Her hands continue shivering as she transfers the rounds to the serving dish. She has to trim the edges, hide them with the icing.

She sets the cake down in the middle of the table. She lays out a serving knife, two forks, two blue green matching plates. She sets out two small rounded snifters. He opens and pours the brandy, slices, serves the cake. They sit across from one another, looking at the cake.

He takes the first bite, closes his eyes.

She says, sorry. It was crumbling at the edges.

He says, I would never notice. It's a thing of beauty.

She says, I wanted it to be perfect.

He says, you know better than to think that way about a thing of beauty.

They talk for a long time. She refills her brandy glass. He cuts another slice of cake. He says, this cake, this cake! He makes her laugh. She drinks her brandy and forgets her imperfections.

She keeps drinking til her vision starts to feel a little wavy.

She says, maybe…do you think that we should call John?

He puts down his glass and looks at her.

I think that we should call him, she says. Just to hear his voice.

He sighs.

I know that isn't what we talked about, she starts to say. She trails off.

He shakes his head.

She looks down.

No, he tells her. Absolutely not.

•

She runs the water for her bath. She drips a few small drops of scented oil, violets and antique roses. Cracks the window. Lilac bushes still in bloom. Crickets still chirping. She looks at the water running, turns the bottle, pours the whole thing in.

She lowers herself in the tub, turns off the water. The house is so quiet, she can hear her husband reading. In another room, the pages crackle, swiftly and distractedly. His chair creaks. Footsteps. Gentle knocking at the door. She says, come in. The door creaks.

He sits on the edge of the toilet. He looks at her, smiling. He says, it's a lovely night.

She nods. A very nice breeze.

He says, do you mind if I read in here?

She says, of course not. She looks at the tile. It's a patternless dispersion of small, thumbnail-sized pink squares.

More pages crackling. What are you reading?

I don't know, he says. *A Farewell to Arms*. I don't really know why.

She thinks, I haven't read that book since high school. She tries to remember what it's like, but she cannot seem to remember anything.

It's all nonsense, he reads. It's only nonsense.

What's nonsense? She says.

I'm not afraid of the rain, he reads in a strange voice that she's never heard.

I'm not afraid of the rain

I am not afraid of the rain.

Oh, oh, God, he says, I wish I wasn't.

She says, is it any good?

He says, it's okay.

Are you going to finish reading it?

He folds the book and puts it down.

He says, look at me.

She tilts her head.

He says, please look at me.

She looks up toward him.

They sit, looking at each other for a long time.

She hears a car drive through their neighborhood, outside.

She hears a dog bark, distantly.

He says, I need to shave.

She says, yes, that's a good idea.

He stands up and looks at himself in the mirror.

Do you mind if I shave while you take your bath?

No, not at all, she says.

She stirs her hand around inside the water, turns her gaze back to the tile. He hums as he lays out all his shaving instruments.

A nice clean shave, he says.

She feels tired. Nice and clean, she says. She lies back, drinking in the scent of violets and roses.

•

She towels off and walks to bed, disrobed. Her skin is shimmering. She pulls the sheets back. She can hear him gargling salt water. He has always done that. She could never bring herself to do it. She says, I'm going to bed, now.

He says, just a minute, dear.

He spits. He rinses. He turns off the light. Moon rays shine through the blinds. He stands beside the closet, unbuttoning and undressing.

He stands naked, for a moment. He regards her. White hair, soft like milkweed feathers. Small breasts, like the lids of tired eyes.

She regards him. He is still strong, though his skin is strangely delicate. Broad shoulders flecked with small, dry, peeling patches.

He says, what do you think I should wear tomorrow?

Light blue shirt, she says. Gray windowpane plaid.

He nods. The day after that?

She says, dark blue, tan slacks. I have ironed them already.

You are wonderful, he says. He puts his clothes into the laundry hamper.

He gets into bed. She feels the halo of his body heat. He breathes in. He breathes out, his halo widening to take her in. Her heart beats faster. Crickets chirping, still. Her heart begins to pound. She reaches for his hand. He holds it firmly in his own.

•

In her dream, they are driving at night, she and her husband. She knows John is in the backseat because she can hear his voice. She cannot hear what he is saying, though. The windows are rolled down. The sound of windswept pavement, rushing, swallowing all of his words. The shadows of the trees stretch out toward them. The lamps lined along the median cast greenish light. A thick, deep fog looms just ahead. John's voice sounds like an angry static, like the sound of tidal waves that crash into the stones with far more force than you imagined.

•

She wakes up to smells of oil frying in the kitchen. She can hear the sound of something sizzling in a pan. She slips into her robe and steps out to the table. She sits down and yawns. Her husband sets a cup of coffee down for her.

She says, thank you.

He kisses her forehead. Toast and scramble.

That sounds nice. She sips her coffee. Just the way she likes it. She hears scuffling and scraping, stove dials clicking, dish ware clanking. You need help? She says.

No thank you, he says. Shit.

What's wrong?

She gets up and she pops the toast. It isn't bad, she says. It's just a little crispy.

Damn it.

She smiles. It doesn't matter, she says.

He does not smile. It does matter, he says.

He puts two new slices in the toaster, using up the loaf. You see? It all works out, he says.

She nods. It all works out.

•

They go to the art museum. They walk through hallways of lit cases, mirrored walls, red velvet ropes, raised platforms of decorative furniture. A gilded fainting couch. A carved ebony chair. A marble tiled mantle with an ornate etched brass screen.

Each article of furniture is labeled with a date, a brief description, and an antique photograph. The photographs reveal the rooms within the old homes that once housed the furniture, homes that were torn apart, or burned into the ground.

They wander through the galleries of modern art. One picture is a plain gunmetal gray reflective surface, through which bits of people—faces, scarves, and shoes—drift back and forth, sharpening, fading, and receding through the dark its reflection, like the surface of a frozen pond.

They walk toward the picture. As they move in closer, other people's movements blur to foggy streaks of light. They see themselves reflected, drawn out from the world for a moment. They stand, looking at this portrait of themselves as they are now.

•

They have dinner at her favorite restaurant, a quiet bistro with a patio in back where no one ever seems to sit. She orders ravioli with leeks, mushrooms, and a light herb sauce. He orders fried eggplant and green tomatoes with a creamy remoulade.

A bottle of wine? He asks.

Just a glass, she says.

He nods. You're right.

She orders white. He orders red.

She smiles. Cheers, I guess.

On the patio, there is a stony fixture that was once a bird bath. Now, it's filled with bits of empty nests and leaves.

The sky fades from pinkish gray to pale blue just as the waiter brings the tray. They eat their dinner very slowly. As she swallows her last bite of ravioli, he sips his last sip of wine, and the sky darkens to the darkest shade of blue.

•

They drive home with the windows rolled down. Her hair drifts into her eyes. The moon is just a sliver through the trees. Her eyes follow the sliver like a shining branch that she will climb out of the forest, into what, she doesn't know.

She realizes she is crying. He says, please. He brushes back her hair. She leans her head into his shoulder.

He rolls the windows up. He runs his fingers through her hair. He whispers, please. You know I'm here. You know I'm here. You know I'm with you.

•

Her husband falls asleep before she does. She lies in bed on her back with her eyes closed, listening to him. He sucks his teeth while he is sleeping, like he's trying to breathe through them. The dull wheezing of his teeth sounds like his footsteps on the stairs.

She dreams that they continue driving through the fog. She cannot hear if John is still with them in the backseat. She cannot see where they are going. She cannot see if her husband is with her. She hears and sees and feels nothing but the fog.

•

She sweeps. She cleans the counters, cleans the dishes. She puts them in boxes in the closet, next to other boxes. She puts labels on the boxes. She arranges them. She stands back and she looks at them. She tries to forget what she put inside.

He cleans their perishable items from the fridge. He holds each item for a moment and considers it, then throws it in a black bag. He throws out

a stale frozen bun
a tub of mayonnaise
a jar of pesto
a jar of brown mustard
an old jar of relish
a new jar of olives
a bottle of dressing
a bottle of white wine vinegar
a lemon
half a jug of milk
half-eaten cake
half of a loaf of bread
left-over casserole
two withered shallots
three slim cloves of garlic
dusts of nameless crumbs

a tub of tapioca pudding
leftover potato salad
and an old potato that is sprouting curls of new green sprigs.

•

After they clean, she wanders off into the bedroom. She takes off her clothes and folds them in the hamper. She stands nude before the full length mirror. He comes into the bedroom and he stands behind her. She watches his reflection undress in the mirror.

You are still beautiful, he says.

She murmurs, still.

You are still beautiful, he says, again. He folds his hands around her waist.

His heavy scent, like salted tea. Her mouth is dry. His hands are somehow moist, but cracked. She licks her lips. She turns around and kisses him.

He kisses her. He strokes her breasts. He bends down to his knees with a familiar gentle groaning, cusps her breasts, and licks the sweat beneath them.

The sun lattices the shades, the curtains drifting. Outside, they can hear a passing plane. Someone is raking, scraping at their lawn.

He kisses underneath her breasts, kisses her breasts, parts her legs with his fingers. She breathes in. She clasps his hand between her legs. She breathes out in small gasps. He kisses in between her legs. He kisses in between his fingertips. He picks her up and carries her to bed.

Their bodies move together with less urgency than they both feel, somewhere deeper in themselves, somewhere that moves them into one another, but prevents them, nonetheless, from moving in effectively. He wraps her tired legs around him and he sighs.

•

She listens as he gargles salt behind the bathroom door. She hears the door creak. She says, wait. She joins him by the bathroom sink. She pours the salt into the spoon, fills up the glass, then pours them both into her mouth at the same time. She tries to make the noise he makes.

Her lips pucker. She gasps. Spits into the sink. She fills the glass, gulps it down desperately. Spits.

Was it as bad as you thought? He says.

She says, yes.

It couldn't be that bad.

She tells him, it was pretty bad, for me.

They wash off at the sink. They brush and floss their teeth.

She sprays on her perfume. He sprays on his cologne.

She brushes and he combs his hair.

They make the bed. They pull their hangers from the closet.

They lay their clothes out on the bed. They stand there for a moment, looking down.

He begins to dress himself. Then, she gets dressed.

•

She opens the drawer and takes out the folders and the envelopes. Arranges them. Her shirt sleeves feel tight around her wrists. She feels pulled together. She looks at him. He looks at the envelopes and nods.

She says, I'm going to call John.

•

Hello, John, she says.

Hello, he says.

She says, I can't talk for long. I just wanted to say hello. How have you been?

All right, he says. Not much has changed. How have you been?

She says, not much has changed.

He says, it's such a nice day, here.

She says, here too. The neighbors burning leaves. The changing colors. I have always loved this time of year.

He says, me too. I've always loved this season too.

There is a pause. She told herself she would not talk beyond the pause, that momentary faltering that always changes their direction.

She says, I really should go. I am sorry, but I need to go.

He says, okay. Well, it was good to hear from you.

It was good talking to you, she says. John, I love you.

He says, I love you too.

She waits. She listens. She can hear the sound of traffic passing through the phone line. From a distance, it sounds like some sort of ghostly whispering. The sound of sirens. They fade off into a quiet whine.

She hopes that somehow she will use these whispers to transmit the thoughts that she cannot and never could articulate.

She says, good-bye, John.

He tells her, good-bye.

She hangs the phone up.

She looks at the gray light of the window and she says, I'm ready.

•

They take one of the envelopes. They take a last look, out the window, look at all the raked and unraked lawns. The bags, the tidy piles, untidy piles, and the burning piles, and the piles of blackened twigs and leaves and ashes.

They hear the otherworldly moaning of the distant train. The humming of the insects, and the straining scent of lilacs. The sounds of laughing, running, crunching leaves, the children playing in their yards. She shuts her eyes. She bites her lip.

They walk into the garage, step into the car. They sit. He pushes down the button that will close the door.

He sighs. He leans back in the seat.

He looks at her. She looks at him, then watches as the wood door slowly lowers itself, unfolding in segments.

The metal edges, creaking, suddenly so unfamiliar.

Her heart shivers with the resonance of the door closing.

All the wood parts and the metal bolts and bits and bands, all straightening themselves into one whole, complete, closed door.

She looks back at her husband. He is looking out the windshield. She looks at him as he looks away, for just a moment.

Then, she looks out of the windshield.

She sits, watching, waiting, as the air grows thick.

She watches as the fog begins to rise.

# AN OPEN ROOM

I've barely left my bed for three days, now. My hair sticks together. I open and close my fingers. I look at the sad pinkish sunlight that filters between them. I look at my fingers and roll on my stomach and groan.

I imagine my insides, your voice. My hands feel slow and charred. The bell tolls, and I hear the distant, muffled screams of children.

Somewhere, somewhere real, there are dunes of white sand and black water. I have seen them. From the kitchen, my tea kettle steams. I ignore it.

Somewhere, somewhere real, there are volcanoes that just sit there. Maybe waiting. Maybe not. I haven't seen them.

There is a lake in here the size of my life, blue-green. What I haven't touched, drowned, is the real story. I bite my lip. My teeth ache. I bite harder, think, *why bother*. I know where things are. I get in the rhythm. It whispers, *why bother, why bother*.

If you were here, you'd hold me down beside the lake.

You'd bend my knees and bend my arms around behind my back.

You'd hold my head down in the water.

I would strain to hear you.

I would listen for you, like the ocean trapped inside a shell.

# ALL OF YOUR MOST PRIVATE PLACES

They drive together through the night. They roll the windows down. The air surrounds them as they're driving through the desert. It's everything. It's what they hear. The wind made by their movement. Wheels on asphalt. Pinkish river-pool of neon lights receding.

It's the city. He turns up the headlights, turning down the radio. The static crackles, gravel, road fades into dust. The road becomes each line of white revealed by the headlights. Great black jaws of mountain swallowing the swimming pools of pink.

She thinks, the city feels like a volcano. It is not the first time she has had this thought. She feels foggy. Sweating. It's the desert heat. Volcano. Neon lava. Or whatever. But, she thinks, there's more to it than that.

You want the radio? He says.

Not really. She's not listening.

He says, me neither. He's not listening. He turns it off.

The city feels dormant in the day. The neon lights are not yet lit, but they're still felt. She feels this pulse. This throb of buildings pumping false metallic air. The cooling which she understands creates a greater heat.

As they drive from the city, she thinks, it is strange just how easy it seems when you're driving away. In the day time, when lights are just rhythms, she feels like the city is all that there is.

•

In the darkness, the desert is always erupting. It's something that everyone knows. It's a looming, their knowledge, these dark crags, this bright neon magma, this charge to the air. The night sky smells like sagebrush, sand, which is to say, this powder, ammunition, dust. The smell of heat. The cactus flowers bloom.

Meanwhile, a line of cars pulls into Station UA1. The station workers scan their cards. The gate goes up and down. A sign above the gate says: An Environmental Research Park. The sign below that says: Buckle up. It's the law.

The workers wait there in their line of cars, sipping their coffee from plastic or tin tubes, styrofoam or paper cups. They check the time. They clear their throats. They yawn. They stretch in place. They sift around in pockets for their ID cards.

They look out of their windows and they wait. Long black lines of lamps cast cold white lines of light.

Their own white jackets sit beside them, folded into rectangles. They wait. They have so many sets of clean white jackets just like these. They sip their coffee, think of stains. These clean white surfaces. Such a responsibility. They think, it is only a matter of time.

They sit there, sipping. The beginning of another day. They think of darkness turning into white, try not to think of stains. They think of home. They think of pulling their clean jackets from the wash. The soft clean smell. They're like spare sheets for some strange guest who never seems to leave.

•

They feel this unnameable dread when he pulls their car into the driveway. It's the sound of splintered blacktop, hissing. Then, the way it stops. The respiration of exhaust, for just a moment. Then, the way it stops completely. Then, the feeling they are home. They have arrived.

They take off their clothes and they mill toward the bedroom. She waits for him by the window, palms flattened against the ledge. She hears him click the light on, so she squints. He comes up from behind. He puts his hands upon her hands and presses her into the glass.

The blonde-lit linen drapes move as their bodies move. The edges stick. She grips the ledge. She looks. She peers outward into the night.

She sees the feathered silhouette of their acacia tree. Then, she sees fog. She squints. Then, fog. Then, branches. Fog. Then, branches. Fog. Then, branches.

She closes her eyes. Her nipples rub against the linen. Sweat gleams on her stomach. She feels like she's floating, falling, into nothingness.

Her hands slip from the ledge. He grabs her hands. He grabs her wrists. He grabs her arms. He grabs her legs. He gasps. He comes.

They lie together on the bed. She's turned toward the window. He clicks off the light. He's turned toward her back.

Good night, my dear, he tells her back.

Good night, she tells the window.

I love you, he tells her back.

I love you too, she tells the window.

•

The tourists turn to face the viewing platform. Its window is the front wall of UA1's so-called bunker. The tour director, Lee, directs them to the glass, assures them it is bullet-proof. The bunker's built to standard. Whatever that means.

Lee distributes small plastic binoculars to the tourists. He directs them to the model subdivision. Rows of square lawns, picket fences, and split-level houses. Built to standard. Desert stretches out on every side.

It's called Survivor City, he explains. The tourists mumur-nod with grave expressions, like this means something to them. The window's amber tinted, so the light looks gold. It frames the subdivision with a soft, uncanny glow.

It has a retro look, a tourist says.

Another tourist says, it's like a 50s photograph. Looks like my mother's neighborhood.

A man in a Hawaiian shirt is really getting into it. He says, I feel like I've stepped back into another time.

Lee shakes his head. He says, it's not another time. It's meant to look like anywhere in any time. Timeless, in other words.

The man says, Lee. He looks at him like, I don't know you. He says, Lee, I think I know what I am feeling when I feel it.

Lee does not respond. He details the history of the museum, the legacy of the test site, the ways that it has changed throughout the years. He leads them through a hallway filled with stainless steel beams, then ducks them down into a tunnel filled with pipes. Some pipes emit a slight sulfuric smell. Please watch your heads, he says, directing them to shelves of safety goggles and hard hats.

The tunnel begins to get dark, but there are head lamps on the hats. The on-switch is on the left side, Lee tells the tourists. Click, click, click, click. The clicking echoes like the dripping of a cavern wall. The dim-lit tunnel flickers like a line of lightening bugs.

Eventually, the tunnel opens out into a larger viewing platform filled with many periscopes. Lee tells the tourists they're invited to look through the periscopes, to get a clearer picture of Survivor City.

Are those people in the houses? Someone inevitably asks.

Lee shakes his head. Test figures. In a minute, I will demonstrate.

The periscopes allow the tourists to peer into the model houses. Through the windows, they can see the ways the figures were arranged.

One model home reveals a set of figures in the living room. Two child-size figures sit together on the love seat. A man-size figure lounges in an armchair by the floor lamp with a glass beside him and a magazine spread on his lap.

A woman figure in a dress stands by the window. She is close enough for tourists to gaze at the details of her face. She wears her hair styled in a simple mid-length bob. She has long, black-lined lashes, blue eyes, and a pale sort of almost-smile.

Survivor City is outlined with huge ominous craters. From this angle, now, within the periscopes, their full scale is revealed. Most craters are the size of many houses. If they panned in closer, in the corner, they would see a tortoise peeking from its shell.

Do they use real nukes? Hawaiian shirt man asks.

Lee says, of course not, no. They don't use nuclear explosives. They have not conducted real tests in decades. Things are different, now, he says. This is a research park. They're simply recreating an experience.

So, they're not real nukes? The shirt man says.

Lee says, they're not. They're meant to look and act as much like real nukes as possible.

Lee does not like to hear himself answer this question. In all honesty, he doesn't know what happens at this site. He's never seen the real testing site, the part that's confidential. When he asked his boss about it, he was vague and cagey.

That's not your job, he said. That part is science. Visitors don't come for science. That is not what they are looking for.

What are they looking for? Lee glanced down at his boss's gun belt, then quickly looked back up into his gleaming metal badge.

They want reassurance. They're just making sense of things, he said. This gives a good face. Humanizes the whole operation.

Lee's boss moved closer, then. He noticed he smelled slightly musky and his breath had just a bit of an acidic tinge. He patted his hand on Lee's shoulder. You do good, he said. You do important work. It is important to preserve our own humanity.

•

He looks across the table at his wife as they eat breakfast, which is flaxseed waffles served with slices of banana. She's arranged the waffles on their avocado green fiesta ware, banana slices laid like petals on the plate.

She is wearing her work clothes, a powder blue shirt dress with buttons buttoned to the neck. It is classy, he thinks. There's a small gap between the two buttons above and right below her breasts. He can see a slight trace of her bra. He thinks that this is sexy. She looks at him while she is sipping her coffee. She raises one eyebrow. He raises one eyebrow. He thinks, she is classy, but sexy.

He has this fantasy. He thinks about it often, but he hasn't brought it up yet. He is waiting for the right time.

He looks down and scrapes his waffles. She gets up and takes the plates. Her heels click. The water hisses. Plates clink. Now is not the right time.

In his fantasy, they find a local call girl from an ad. They call the number. They tell her what they are thinking. She tells them she is excited. She senses they are attractive. Classy/sexy. Something he thinks that call girls are not used to.

This is all part of the fantasy, this need to give her something. They provide the call girl with something exceptional. They're not just there to give her money. She enjoys herself. She feels relaxed. They talk together and they listen to some music.

He pours champagne. When the call girl finishes her glass, she gets a look. She leans in toward his wife and starts unbuttoning her dress. Her eyes are on that gap between the buttons. The call girl is wearing something slutty, something that his wife would never wear.

He asks, is it okay if I take pictures? She says, yes, of course. Please feel free. As many as you need. He snaps a picture of the girl unbuttoning his wife's dress, panning in on her expression, capturing her smile. He takes a picture of them kissing as their bodies fold together, capturing her smile as it melts in someone else's mouth.

•

Lee says, now, count down from 10. The tourists glance up, back, and forth. They clutch their wrists. Hawaiian shirt man's dripping sweat. 10, 9, 8, 7, 6, 5, 4, 3, 2, 1. Silence. Light. Explosion.

They see the flash before they hear the sound, which is so deep, it barely registers as what they know it is. There is a second flash. The shutters and the roof tops seem to splash in one direction, riding on the arc of an invisible wave.

The windows shatter. Paint begins to blister, bubble, singe. The edges of the roof are licked with tiny temporary flames. The flames burn quickly. All the houses stand just as they stood. It is a testament to standards, Lee says, how well they were built.

The tourists look out through the periscopes. They see the figures in the houses were not harmed. Although, the fringes of the woman's bangs are black. Her lashes charred and feathered. Bits of glass gleam on her shoulders like scattered necklace.

One of the children now leans to the side, like she is pulling back. The man leans forward, like he's doubled over in some kind of shock. What does this mean, they think, this delicate destruction? Tourists file toward the exit. They do not know what this means.

They fiddle with their pamphlets. Thanks and come again. You're welcome. They came here to learn something. They don't remember. They leave, feeling they've learned nothing. They pull out onto the desert highway, turn the AC up, turn on the radio. Hawaiian shirt man says, it was a museum. That is how they did things in the past. His wife nods and the desert stretches all around them. He says, honestly, we've come a long way. The sun glares. He adjusts the mirrors. He smiles at his wife. They are relieved, but disappointed.

•

There is a moment in her drive to work that always catches her. It is the moment where the highway meets the turn-off to the desert. It's the turn-off that they take on their long night drives. She has never driven on this desert route during the day.

She thinks of driving through the desert to wherever. Gnarled scraps of brush and cactus trees, cracked spiderwebs of dirt becoming graceful slopes of dunes, becoming sky, becoming nothing, nothing but potentialities that she cannot envision.

•

Instead, she pulls off at the donut shop. She buys two mixed dozens and a box of coffee. The pink cardboard sits beside her. Its smells sweet and sticky. Sticking her to what she needs to do and where she needs to go.

What does she need to do? Where does she need to go? She barely knows, these days, but it involves getting their coffee and their donuts. She deposits them onto a table in the break room with a note. Please take one, says the note. She draws a smiley face. The smiley face's eyes are spread too far apart. She feels that this makes it look a little crazed and desperate.

At her desk, she edits photos of rich people at events. She blurs and touches up and does what's needed to make them look good. Most of the women wear these shelf-like strapless dresses. They look stupid. They're intended to be flattering, but everyone looks fat. Nobody understands themselves, she thinks, fixing the images. She thinks, it's posturing. The things they do to make themselves look classy.

•

He looks out onto an overwatered golf course. He can hear the sprinklers run throughout the day. He forgets them for short intervals while sending e-mails, processing new data, or setting reminders on his calendar. After awhile, he pauses and looks out of the window. He hears three sprits of water, a short revolution, six thin sprits of water, then a revolution, then one longer, louder stream of water, then a revolution, back to the beginning.

Sometimes, he looks beyond the golf course to the mountains, which stand, looking back at him, above the false green slopes. In the morning, they're violet flickers emerging from lavender clouds. By mid-day, they've unfolded a gold-green expanse that recedes into shadows of blue. By the end of the work day, the sky has accumulated a thick yellowish haze. He powers down, flicks off the lights, and stands to close the blinds. He thinks, I have changed through the years in all these ways I can't articulate. The mountains always still themselves, a looming gray suggestion.

•

As a child, he spent a lot of time inside his best friend's partially finished basement, on the unfinished side, exploring stacks of Playboys. They both sat on these rickety metal-frame lawn chairs. They drank Diet Rite because that's what they had. The crushed cans piled up. The basement smelled like dirty socks.

He was filled with a sense of discovery then. It had little to do with the images. The women were okay, but they mostly looked the same. The pictures blended with the sound of turning pages. The sense of discovery came from the things that they found themselves saying.

I like that one, his friend pointed out. I like when they have puffy nipples.

Puffy? He said.

Yeah, his friend said. When they look like that.

He asked, what do you call them, then, when they're not puffy?

I don't know. He shrugged. He crushed his can. Just regular, I guess.

I like that one, he said. The red lace panties.

His friend nodded his approval. Yeah. All girls look good in red.

I guess they do, he thought. He spent a silent moment thinking, why? I like how bright it is, he said. It just stands out.

This way, they both established their taxonomy of parts, their lexicon for subtle preferences in color, size, and shape.

•

While driving home, he thinks of Diet Rite and red lace panties. He thinks about his wife, how she is beautiful. He's lucky. He wants to share that sense of mutual discovery. He wants to see what she sees, create a shared language.

•

As a child, his wife was frightened of discovery. She was a quiet girl. That's what her mother said. She preferred empty spaces; after all, she lived within the desert. She should've been able to be happy where she was.

It doesn't work like that, her mother said. She told her, in a perfect world. She sighed, of course, because the world wasn't perfect. She felt her pocket with the lipstick and the box of cigarettes. She pulled two sticks of spearmint gum out of the other pocket. In a perfect world, we'd all get what we want, she said, but we don't really even know exactly what we want, most of the time.

Her mother took her swimming. She'd swim while her mother lounged beside the pool. She crawled out of the pool whenever she felt hungry. Pool water seems to designed to make you hungry, she complained. Her mother told her to be patient. She was happy lying in the sun. She tried to lie there with her mother, but her body felt exposed, so she turned over on her stomach, spread a towel on her back. She felt her stomach pinched between the plastic chair slats. She looked through the space between the slats and watched a spider drowning in a puddle.

She went to slumber parties where they looked at magazines. The magazines asked questions about what they wanted, who they could become. Could you be a model? The magazine articles asked. Could I be a model? The girls at the parties would ask themselves. They didn't know. It seemed like a good question.

They stashed the pizza boxes in a greasy corner by the trash. They dug around the junk drawer with this stupid urgency. They found the measuring tape tucked inside an old tin can of cookies from the days when cookies always came in old tin cans.

The girls lined up—they actually lined up—and a girl would measure ankles, wrists, waists, leg length, shoulder width, hips, height, and neck circumference, comparing their measurements to lists of model ranges in the magazines, the standard units used within the industry.

As it turned out, none of them could have been models. Some girls came close in some ways but fell short in others. They were tall enough, but their hips were too wide. Their waists were small enough, but they had scrawny calves or weird thick ankles. Their shoulder width, hips, waist, were all in perfect ratio, but for some reason, one leg was a little longer than the other.

•

While driving home, she thinks of how she hates her insecurities. They're childish, of course. They haven't changed since childhood. She contemplates this concept, childhood. When did it end? She looks out at the endless desert, thinking that it never did.

•

Meanwhile, something horrible is happening at the test site. Not UA1. The real site, the site that uses nukes. They're building new machines that detonate from deep within the earth. Enormous black cables extend in all directions.

These new machines do not leave cratered surfaces. These new machines do not create plume clouds of dust. The explosions of these new machines appear to be invisible. Their damage—unseen and unreachable—is hard to estimate.

Somewhere inside the night, the figures of a man and woman wait inside a model bedroom in a model home. The man lies, turned toward the woman's back, his arms around her waist. The woman lies, turned toward the window, palms clasped underneath her head.

Good night, my dear, the male figure tells the woman's back.

Good night, the woman figure tells the model window.

Good night, the long black cable tunnels whisper through inaudible uncanny tremors they can somehow hear.

I love you, he tells her back.

I love you too, she tells the window.

I love you too, the long black cable tunnels tell them. As the neon glow begins to rise, the summer insects drone. The long black cable tunnels swarm with the unseen.

•

As a child, Lee only liked to masturbate in bed. Whenever he came, he would wipe the leavings underneath his bed frame. He was not sure why he did this, but he didn't think to stop, once he began. It was a ritual that had to be fulfilled.

One day when Lee came home from school, he saw his mother crouched beside the bed, wearing an apron and a pair of yellow gloves. Her gloved hands reached beneath the mattress, scrubbing down the frame. White soapy streams of something dripped into a metal bucket.

He said nothing. She said nothing, even when she finished cleaning, but she placed a box of tissues on his bedside table.

That night, as he drifted off to sleep, he listened to the sounds of traffic curving through a nearby stretch of highway. He felt empty, in his bed. His bed felt empty and he thought about the bucket, being filled with little bits of him. He closed his eyes. He didn't understand why he felt lonely. He had not imagined how much he could miss his own accumulation.

•

Lee lies in bed now thinking of the real test site thinking how his thoughts are now this fear that slowly seeps and builds into this feeling that explodes when he's alone inside the darkness and attaches itself permanently to the underside of his bed.

•

Tonight, they are having sex in bed. They tangle their sand-colored sheets into the shapes of miniature dunes. He twists her legs around him, bends her knees, lifts them and lowers them. She lifts herself and lowers herself down. She sweeps her hands along the mini sand dunes. Sweat sticks to his forehead. She licks it. He kisses her. She accidentally butts his chin.

They lie in bed. He's looking at her back. She's looking at the window and they almost fade into the old routine. But there's this feeling in his stomach, this electric buzz that shocks him intermittently. It's giving him a sense of clarity. Now is the time. He says, I have this fantasy. His wife turns over in bed and she faces him. She gives her full attention.

•

15 minutes later, she is standing in front of the vanity. She's rubbing cotton balls of creamy liquid on her body. He says, look, we do not

have to do this. We don't have to do this right away. She's rubbing really, really frantically.

He says, are you okay?

She looks back in the mirror. I'm fine.

He rolls his eyes.

She says, I'm fine.

He repeats, we don't have to do this.

She throws down her cotton ball. It's hard to throw dramatically. She covers her face with both her hands and cries.

She says, I'm sorry. No, I want to. No, I do, I promise.

After a minute, she says, is it me, or is it *really* hot?

•

It is really hot that night. A couple miles away, a homeless woman passes out beside a dumpster in an alley. The last thing she sees before she dies is dumpster lid. The last thing she smells is a heat wave of dumpster rising up into her face.

Nobody sees her. No one knows her when they find her. No one calls to claim connection to her body or her life.

•

15 minutes later, they are looking at the laptop in bed, clicking through the profiles on various escort sites. The women are categorized into Blonde, Brunette, Asian, Redhead, and Ebony. Some escort profiles are labeled as product descriptions. The product descriptions make promises. One product promises, if you look into her eyes, you'll fall prey to her sweet spell of seduction. One product promises she has an unmatched appetite for sexual experiences beyond your wildest dreams. One product promises she'll make those dreams reality, says she will gladly listen to whatever you desire. She says she will go to all of your most private places. She says she will fulfill you, physically and mentally.

•

The next morning, she absently chews on a donut while editing photos. She is editing a picture of an average-looking woman. She licks powdered sugar from her lips and analyzes which features construct this average-looking woman's averageness.

The woman's wearing average-looking clothes (a shelf-like strapless dress.) The woman wears an average-looking hairstyle (artificially straightened bob.) The woman has an average-seeming body, not too thin or heavy, not too short or tall (she could be wearing heels beneath her dress.) The woman has some pretty features (full lips, high cheekbones,) some noticeable flaws (a weak jawline, an oddly upturned nose.) She looks down at her empty napkin, wondering when and how she came to be the arbiter of who and what is average.

•

He goes to the office bathroom to look in the mirror. It is a private bathroom. You must have a key to get inside. This privacy affords him time. He doesn't need much time. He studies his eyes, nose, and mouth, evaluates his jawline, lifts his shirt and turns, moves close, steps back, and makes a couple different faces. He nods. Just as he expected, he's an average-looking man.

•

When they come home from work, they view more escort profiles. They notice one they both like called Leelani. In her pictures, she is wearing red lace panties. She is posing in the gold-lit glow of what appears to be a luxury hotel.

I like that one, he tells her. The red lace panties.

His wife nods. All girls look good in red. She presses her red lips together.

Puffy nipples, too, he says.

His wife nods.

Perky breasts.

She nods. The profile mentions she's a spinner. Do you know what that means?

He says, a spinner is a petite girl. She's really light. Easy to spin on your cock.

She looks blank. He doesn't know what her expression means.

He explains, you can switch from front to back without needing to pull out.

She says, oh. She now knows what a spinner is.

There is a level to this research she enjoys. In many ways, it is an interesting inversion of her job. She smiles for him but he doesn't see her smile. The laptop glow reflects into his glasses, turning them to silent screens.

•

Leelani lives in a month-to-month rental on the other side of the city. Leelani is not this woman's real name. She is not the woman in the pictures, either. She's a woman with a couple features comparable to the pictures.

She is one of three women the agency currently uses to portray the part of Leelani. These women come and go. Leelanis come and go.

In this moment, she is out of character, crouched on her bed. She's watching *Die Hard* on a grainy television screen. She's in her underwear, which is a pair of blue-striped cotton Hanes and a white t-shirt with a city name she has no real connection to.

She is painting her nails a shade of dark shimmery slate blue. The name of the polish she uses is Tough As Nails. She thinks about an article she read once—she can't recall where—about nails, how nails, hair, and skin are all made of the same thing.

She blows on her nails and they bristle. Her hair stands on its edges. Yippie ki yay, motherfuckers, she whispers into the static.

She waves her hands to dry them. Something's creeping in her stomach. Hunger. Loneliness. Who knows. She swallows hard.

She waves her fingers back and forth like little wings. Her nails look good.

She smiles as the helicopter explodes.

•

It's called Survivor City, Lee tells a new crowd. The new group nods. A new Hawaiian shirt man queries him about the nukes. They're meant to look and act as real as possible, he now explains. They now look through the periscopes into another room.

It is a bedroom with a man and woman lying in their bed. The woman's turned toward the window, looking out at them. Her gaze now meets the tourists' gaze. Some tourists back off from the periscopes. The scene looks too familiar, feels too voyeuristic.

•

Her fantasy is simple. She tells herself it's simple. She tells herself she has no expectations.

She has expectations. Everybody does.

Okay, she knows.

Okay, she tells herself, maybe it's not that simple.

In her fantasy, the call girl's pretty in a different way from her.

But not too pretty.

Not too different.

It's hard to explain.

She's pretty in a way that they can both relate to, but they both relate to her in separate, different, and unspoken ways.

She looks at her like, we're both women, and that means something.

She doesn't know what it means, what it should mean, what she wants for it to mean.

She knows she doesn't want the call girl to be prettier than her. She doesn't want to look at her and feel inferior.

She wants to feel attraction to her and connection with her and she wants her husband to experience attraction and connection.

But she wants a firm before, during, and after, a firm cut off, for her husband to feel, afterward, they both have everything they need.

•

He calls the agency from his car on his lunch break. A woman answers, asks what she can do for him. She has just a hint of an accent he can't trace. He tells her that he wants to book Leelani.

Is she available tonight? He asks.

She says, please hold on, darling. Just a moment. He can hear another phone ring in the background. He hears her shuffle, pick up, and the muffled vagueness of her voice. A moment later, shuffle, pick up, she returns.

Yes, dear, she says. Thank you for waiting. Yes, she can see you tonight.

What are her rates? He asks. The website doesn't specify.

250 gets her there and comfortable, she says. Whatever happens after that is up to you, of course.

The pictures on the site, he clears his throat. The pictures on the site- are those an accurate reflection of what she looks like?

An accurate reflection, she repeats. Her voice sounds like it's smiling. Absolutely, yes, of course. I should be honest though. We use a model photograph, she says. We use a model to protect the girls. Their privacy, she says.

He says, I understand.

Our girls are beautiful, she says. Leelani is a classy lady, much more beautiful and lovely than a picture.

I have another question, he says. Does she work with couples?

Let me check, she says. He hears more shuffling and another muffled voice. The phone receiver rustles against something when her voice returns. She tells him, yes. She sounds excited to deliver the good news.

I am booking a date with my wife, he explains.

Ah, she says. That will be good. The pitch of her voice rises. And your wife, she says, does she like pretty ladies?

He thinks for a moment. Yes, she does, he says.

Leelani is a pretty lady, she says. Very pretty. He provides his address and he books the date.

That's good. You and your wife are going to have a good time, she says. Can I do anything else for you? Baby? She adds, a bit too late.

He pauses. Yes, he realizes. Can she wear something specific?

Of course, baby, she says. This time it sounds much more natural.

Please ask her to wear red lace panties, he says.

Absolutely. Red lace panties, she repeats. I will have her wear them for you.

He hangs up and unwraps his take-out salad in the car. He peels off the plastic lid, peels off a second sealed layer. He tears the dotted line along the dressing packet, pours it on, and stirs it through the salad with a plastic spork. The salad is okay. He squeezes out more dressing. He chews slowly, moving bits of every bite he takes inside his mouth. The texture feels weirdly uniform. Well, what does he expect? He thinks, that is the key: adjust your expectations.

•

She gets home early and she walks into the bedroom. She pulls three dresses from the closet, spreads them out across the bed. She then arranges them with corresponding objects, panties, stockings, garter belts, and different pairs of matching heeled shoes.

She stands against the closet door to contemplate the dresses. She thinks they look like little shadow people. They're waiting for a human form to fill them, to make sense of them. They're waiting for a human form to be fulfilled.

She looks and can't remember when or where she wore these dresses. She looks and feels like she's never seen them. She feels like they all belong to separate shadow bodies. Faceless, featureless. Unknown, unknowable.

•

Lee says, now, count down from 10. The tourists glance up, back, and forth. The figures in the bedroom wait there, helplessly. 10, 9, 8, 7, 6, 5, 4, 3, 2, 1. Silence. Light. Explosion.

Something goes wrong. Something has gone wrong and the house goes up. The flicker flames burst into streamers into banners into clouds of billow bulbs of terrible terrific toxic fire. The whole house is engulfed. The tourists gasp. Is this a test? Is this supposed to happen?

Lee's eyes widen. He grabs for a phone against the wall. He speaks a numbered code. A muffled voice says, yes. It will be dealt with.

Lee instructs the tourists to please remain calm. Yes, yes, of course, this is a test. There is no need to worry. They are miles from the fire. Remember, when you look into the periscope, the things you see appear much closer to you than they really are.

The fire burns out on its own within a couple minutes. Where the house stood, there is now a crater pit of blackened smoke and dust. The crater is the only evidence that anything existed. In this space, the only evidence is absence.

The figures in the bedroom were just models, Lee reminds them. The house was just a model. Nothing in the house was real. The objects were not used. The rooms within its walls were untouched, once they were arranged. In short, he says, nothing about the house was human.

Inside the crater, tiny shapes are drifting, shapes and movements that the tourists' periscopes all fail to reveal. The shapes are skeletons of desert creatures, lizards, mice, and squirrels that made nests, made their own families within the model home.

•

She runs a bath. She stands behind the sink and stares into the mirror. She watches her reflection turn to vapors. Now, her face is just this foggy, vaguely colored pixellation. She thinks, somewhere, on some level, this is what I always am.

She gets into the hot bath and she tries to feel sexy. She is hoping that the haze of heat will turn her on. She lathers soap between her fingers, thinks of pin-up photos of rich naked ladies with their nearly naked soapy-bubbled servants.

She drifts down deeper in the bath. The steamy water swirls. She breathes in, thinking of the preparations to be made. She thinks about how sex is getting clean, then getting dirty, getting clean, then getting dirty, on and on for your whole fucking life.

•

Meanwhile, Leelani prepares for their date. She too stands by the closet, pulling dresses and assessing them. Her choice is simple, though, as she has fewer options. All her clothes are either sexy clothes (for work) or lounging clothes (for private life.)

Leelani's private life does not resemble her profile. She mostly lives in bed, but that is incidental. She lives with a fan positioned toward the corner of the mattress where she crouches, watching television while she paints her nails.

•

She's putting on her lipstick by the mirror when he comes home. Bright red, of course. She dabs, purses her lips, and smiles at him.

She says, how was your day? It is a day like any other and it makes no difference what they're doing in a couple minutes.

He says, okay, and puts a bag of groceries on the counter. In the bag of groceries, there's a bottle of champagne. They do not drink.

She asks, so, what's the bottle for? She doesn't ask him, who.

He shrugs. I don't know. It's just classy, right, to have champagne?

She's putting on mascara, so she's making a strange face. She keeps her eyes wide open as she brushes them behind the mirror. She thinks, we all do stupid things to seem attractive. She says, classy, yes. You're right. It's good to have something to offer.

I made a mix, he says, to play while we, you know.

She nods.

He says, I'm going to play the first few tracks, make sure it sounds okay.

He plays the first track. It's a sexy R&B song filled with bass and female back-up vocalists whose voices sound too shimmery.

He moves beside her in the mirror. He smiles and combs his hair. He unbuttons his shirt, sprays on cologne. He says, and, well?

She says, I don't know.

He says, what.

She says, eh.

He says, what.

She says, it's just. I don't know.

He says, what.

She says, it's just kind of intense. It sounds like you're trying to say something.

He buttons up his shirt. She screws the cap on her mascara.

He looks at her in the mirror. His look says, Jesus Christ. Give me a break.

We won't play music then, he says. No problem. Done.

Okay, she says.

It doesn't matter anyway, he says.

Okay, she says.

I'm going to brush my teeth, he says. My mouth tastes like a dumpster.

•

He brushes his teeth three times. His mouth just tastes so weird. He puts on more cologne. Why does he smell like shit tonight?

He clears his throat. He says, hey, look. His wife sits by him on the toilet. He says, I called the agency. The profile photo is a model.

She says, what does that mean?

He says, I'm not exactly sure. I just know she might look a little different from her photo.

She thinks of her job, the pictures that she edits. She says, oh.

He says, I know.

She shrugs. She says, I guess we'll see.

He nods in agreement. Yeah. I guess we'll see.

They hover there together, breathing in the scent of his cologne.

•

The agency calls. He picks up.
    She says, Leelani's driving over. She'll be there in five minutes.
    He tells her, thank you.
    He puts the champagne on the table. He straightens the sheets. He says, dear, when the doorbell rings, please answer it for me, okay?
    She tells him, sure.
    He clears his throat. He swirls his spit around his mouth. His mouth tastes awful. He goes back into the bathroom and brushes his teeth.

•

Lee drives home through the desert. The gray sky turns lavender, then violet black. In the distance, he hears thunder as the sky becomes the sand, the road, the hills, the trees. The sky turns everything to shadows except for the white dashed line that separates the road.
    The rain begins to pour. The white line, what he needs to follow, dashed against the road, a dotted line, a slit across the desert's throat. He thinks of long black cable tunnels, veins of toxic blood. He feels the underworld pulsing, pouring out into the open air.
    Lee bites his lip. He wants to close his eyes as he pulls up into the mountains' mouth, the bright pink maw that is the city where he lives. The flashing signs, the buildings streaked with horizontal light incisions, liquid neon drizzles, gushing neon fountains. The palm trees are black silhouettes against the light, fronds blowing in the wind like charred hair, skirts, and flailing arms of captive women.
    The lightning mingles with the neon. An electric sky. The city turns into a brilliant, burning, blazing bulb. The lightning plumes, conducting who knows what within the clouds. A lightening sky. The roots of some inverted flaming bush.
    He parks his car. He locks the door. He holds his keys. Ignores his neighbor, slumped as usual against the slanted staircase. He unlocks

the door. He locks the door. Turns on the light. Ignores the humming strip. Takes off his clothes. Turns off the light. Gets into bed.

For just one sacred moment, all is dark and all is silent. His room is his world, his own deep bluish sanctuary.

But then, the light seeps in. The rainbow light, reflected in the raindrops on the window. Sounds of rain against the glass. The sound of sirens. They remind him that the world goes on and on without him and he lives alone, alone, alone, alone.

•

The doorbell rings. She gets up. She looks through the peephole. There's a short thin woman standing by herself on her front door step. Her hand's clasped around her arm. Her tall shoes teetering. She looks up, back, and forth. She shifts her purse. She shifts her feet. Her hair is wet.

Leelani? She asks.

Yes, she says. They exchange nods.

Come in, she says. She opens up the door. The woman comes inside the house.

She looks at Leelani. She looks nothing like her picture. She seems shorter and less evenly proportioned. She has dark rings underneath her eyes she's tried to hide with makeup. She has dozens of ambiguous tattoos.

She isn't unattractive. She is not someone who would stand out as unattractive in a picture she was editing at work. But she is also not someone who would stand out, especially. But here she is, standing in front of her inside her home, right now.

She hears her husband spit behind the bathroom door. She says, hello.

Leelani nods. Hello. How are you doing, tonight?

She says, I'm fine, thanks. She looks down. Please sit down, she suggests.

Leelani sits down in the middle of the sofa.

She says, would you like some champagne?

No thanks, says Leelani. I don't drink when seeing clients.

She thinks, oh. I am a client. Oh, of course, she says.

She hears the water run, then stop. The bathroom door opens.

Hello, her husband says.

Leelani says, hello.

Her husband sits down in the arm chair. He looks at his wife like, you're still standing. Go sit down. She sits next to Leelani. Looks like you caught the rain, her husband says.

Leelani nods. Storms are so sudden here, she says. They come so strong and then they vanish, just as quickly as they came.

You're not from here? Her husband asks.

She smiles. No, I haven't been here long.

He asks, where are you from?

She shrugs. Around. All over.

Leelani glances back and forth at each of them.

She says, so, I'm assuming you guys haven't done this before?

It's our first time, he nods. And, what about you? Is this your first time, he adds, visiting a couple?

Leelani smiles like she thinks he's trying to deflect. It's not, she says. I've been with other couples before you.

She's trying not to notice that Leelani's hair smells overwhelmingly of hairspray, cheap perfume, and cigarettes.

Leelani says, so, I don't know how much the agency explained. The way this works is, you give me $250, and that gets me here. Now that I'm here, we'll talk about what you've been thinking, and I'll give you prices for the other services you'd like.

He looks at Leelani. Leelani looks at him. He thinks, her face looks blank. He feels off. He wanted her to like him. He feels disappointed. His wife thinks she looks expectant, but she's trying to conceal this behind a blankly feigned expression.

He says, just a moment. I'll go get the money from the bedroom.

She says, take your time, please. I am in no hurry.

•

She looks nothing like the photos, he says.

I am sorry, sir, a woman says. It is a different woman from the agency. Did they explain the photos are a model? We try to choose photos that look as much like our girls as possible.

But, that's the problem, he says. She looks nothing like the photos.

She says, tell me what the woman in the photos looked like.

He describes the woman in the photos. She describes Leelani. She reiterates, one at a time, the features he described.

She says, I don't see how this woman isn't what you're looking for.

He just stands in silence, wishing he could break something.

The woman tells him, in a perfect world.

He interrupts, I know.

She says, give her a chance. I think you'll like her. She's a classy lady.

•

He stands in front of Leelani and pulls $250 from his pocket. She says, thank you, quickly counts the money, puts it in her purse. She says it simply, like a woman in a restaurant addressing the waiter who has just arrived to fill her glass.

He then relays the shortened version of what he was looking for. He tells his fantasy: a threesome, taking pictures. He leaves out the parts about Leelani's mutual excitement, about giving her something. The parts that matter to him.

Leelani says, no pictures. Sorry, I'm not comfortable with that. Everything else sounds great! She names her price. He pays.

He realizes he's been standing this whole time. His wife has inched a little closer. She's holding Leelani's hand.

•

She takes off her dress she helps take off her dress brushes back her hair cigarettes kissing her mouth tasting smoke but she's soft lips smooth skin kissing shoulder sweat lotion she licks pulling down struggle pulling off clasps snipping here let me help sorry no kissing no it's okay he is naked already his cock in her mouth she takes off all the rest of her clothes and her clothes as she sucks on his cock so she kisses her back tastes like sweat sweeps her hair to the side tastes like cigarettes tattoos the moving of fragments of figures she kisses she sees there's a small pinkish bite she bites down on her nipple a bit licks the tip of his cock which is everywhere somehow he fucks her she's kissing her forehead she sucks on her tits she makes noises that sound fake he fucks her she grabs her she grabs her she grips on her hips she makes noises he grabs her she grabs at him trying to hold him she hears something jingle she's wearing an anklet or something it jingles and jingles and jingles they grab for each other they kiss and they kiss her they grab for each other around her and through her she jingles and moans and he fucks and she grabs and she bites and she moans and he moans and he moans and he comes.

•

She walks her to the door, wearing her dress half-zipped, no underwear. Her hair sticks to her neck. She probably looks awful. They walk out onto the front step, which is wet and cool, though the air feels steamy and impatient, pushing them apart.

Leelani feels her pocket with the box of cigarettes. She pulls two sticks of gum out of the other pocket. Want some?

No thank you, she says. She smiles and Leelani smiles back.

Leelani says, I need some money for the cab. $25 should be okay.

She thinks, but I don't think you took a cab. She thinks, whatever. She says, sure. She steps inside, grabs $30 from her purse. She pulls her makeup compact from the purse and takes a look. She thinks, it's not that bad. I've looked better and I've also looked a lot worse.

She gives the money to Leelani. Thanks, she says. She takes the money. Counts it quickly. Zips it up into her purse.

There's traffic on the highway, still. The sounds of humming, splashing, and occasional horns punctuate the distance.

She hears something that sounds like it could be thunder, but the sound is strangely menacing and feels out of place. She looks at

Leelani. She looks so small, even in her heeled shoes. They're silent for a moment. She says, softly, will you be okay?

Leelani squints. She pulls her purse in tight against her body. She says, yeah, I'll be okay. Thank you for everything. Good night.

She understands this is her cue to leave. She steps back. Good night, she says. I'll be in here, she replies, as if she needs to say that.

Back inside, she sees her husband has popped open the champagne. His face is scrunched up like he swallowed something bad. He pours his glass out, puts it down, and cups his hands under the sink. He splashes water in his mouth. He gargles, spits, and slumps into a chair.

That was a fucking waste of grapes, he says. He looks at her. She feels herself trying hard to make her face turn blank.

•

Lee lies in bed, asleep. He's dreaming of the houses in the desert, of the figures lying silent in their rooms. Within his dream, the desert's burning, and the houses are on fire, and the city's a volcano overflowing, and the sky is black.

The city burns. The desert burns. The figures burn. The palm trees burn. The lava pools over them and burns and burns and burns until the rain pours down like hissing needles and it puts the fires out and hardens, washing away every trace of life.

•

He turns on the fan in the bedroom and she turns toward the window, thinking, all our pillows smell like cigarettes.

The fan says whirr-rr, whirr-rr, whirr-rr, click, whirr-rr, whirr-rr, whirr-rr, click, whirr-rr, whirr-rr, whirr-rr, click, whirr-rr, whirr-rr, whirr-rr.

She sees a timed light turning on inside the neighbor's house. Between their windows, it takes on a murky luminescence. Like the milky little world viewed inside a fish tank.

Whirr-rr, whirr-rr, whirr-rr, click, whirr-rr, whirr-rr, whirr-rr, click.

•

Leelani drives across the city, windows down. She breathes into the air. The rain has stopped. She lights a cigarette. Raindrops leftover from the storm. They're clinging to her windshield. They reflect the light like multicolored haloes.

The sound of tires on wet asphalt makes her feel lonely. She turns on the radio. She glances at her cigarette. This little nub of burning tar, this stick of glowing ash. The radio plays songs about women that no one understands.

You must not know bout me.
You must not know bout me.
You must not know bout me.
You must not know bout me.

She thinks, it's strange to be desired, but not really wanted. Not even desired, maybe. It depends on what desire means. It changes. She breathes smoke. She thinks, it changes. And she's getting older. Fuck. It doesn't matter. We're all gonna die.

She thinks, a city in the desert. What a dumb idea. Whose idea was it? What a crazy place to live. She thinks, I like this city, though. I like the way it feels. To be desired, but unwanted. To be going somewhere, there, then gone.

Her wrists look thin and bluish as she grips the steering wheel. It's a disappearing act. She's getting good at this. A city in the desert. Who lives there? Who's capable of living there? She thinks, I am. I'm living there. She thinks, yes, I belong here.

•

Meanwhile, the mountains are the same black jagged things they always are. The desert is the same vast gray expanse. The air hangs like a hiss between the sky, the asphalt, as the pinkish pool of neon light stirs softly in the distance.

Somewhere within the desert, there are bodies strewn and charred. Somewhere within the desert, there are bones of bodies buried. Some knowledge of them drifts through here, some sense of the unknowable, some shimmering that fades into some shiver on the air.

The dark smells of the desert rise into this shiver. Sagebrush, sand, which is to say, this powder, ammunition, dust. The air, with all its dust, with everything it carries, moves the way it always does.

The cactus flowers bloom into the night.

# THINGS WE SAY WE SEE

You see a half-collapsed old house with green-tinged, rusted roofs. I see a flock of vultures circling something in the woods.

You see a pretty lady with a haircut I would like. I see an old man with an old small dog that looks just like him.

You see a train. I see a tree. You see a sign. I see a flag. You see a star.

I see a shape that doesn't have a name.

I tell you, look!

And you say, look! And I say, look! And you say, look!

And I say, look! And you say, look!

And I don't see it.

## INDOOR/OUTDOOR

The houses in the hills are bad at being real, thinks the younger sister, looking out the back car window. They all look sad, she thinks, all spread apart, connected by their flimsy trails, clumsy, ragged roads like scratches.

If they were houses on a map, they would not look so sad, she thinks. They would be white dots, little speckles on the green. If they were houses in a model village, they'd be small, white boxes, like the ones beneath the glass-framed landscape at the rest stop. The white houses looked happy there. At least, they made her happy, looking at them, and imagining their insides. She did not picture people living in them, though. Instead, she pictured different kinds of food, white boxes filled with carry-out.

Maybe that's why the houses in the hills are bad at being real. They are not like boxes, or, at least, not like the ones in diagrams. They look uneven, badly folded, badly balanced on the hills, and she can tell by looking she would not like what's inside.

The younger sister says, does anybody live in there?

Yes, says the mother. There are people who live in the hills, in many different places, who live different lives from ours. She smiles, thinking, it is time for us—at last—to talk about these things.

No one responds.

The younger sister looks back out the window like she's disappointed that the mother's said something so obvious. Meanwhile, the hills build into mountains and the sad scratch trails grow more sparse, as do the yards of all the small white houses.

The houses all grow dingier and dingier, the scratches, somehow thinner, but somehow more scratched, more savage.

Such different lives, the mother says, in case the father's listening.
She glances to her left.
He isn't listening.

•

The father's driving. He is focused on his driving. He has driven for six hours and they have six more to go. His eyes are tired, but they're focused on his driving, and his eyes and ears need to stay focused, so they do not leave the main road.

*In one mile*, says the GPS, *turn left on Sacramento*, and the father smiles at the GPS's voice.

It is a low-tone female robot British accent—that says, *Sah-crah-mehn-to*—that he has selected for its sexual appeal.

•

The older sister also isn't listening to her. She has her headphones on and she is listening to Frank Ocean. The soft guitar palms through her, shimmering its muted, misty halo, in its jangled gauze that drapes around his voice.

*I thought that I was dreaming when you said you loved me.*
*It started from nothing. I had no chance to prepare.*
*I couldn't see you coming.*

She thinks that maybe, she will see someone that she could not see coming. She cannot see much around her, now. The sun sets, sky dims. She repeats the song. She's looking at the dark line as it bleeds into the bar along the screen.

She trains her eyes along the dark line as the song plays.
She repeats the song.
Repeats the filling in of this dark line.
She's waiting to be filled, to fill the dark space this song represents.
She waits. She listens, looks into the landscape of his voice.

•

Before the summer, when the older sister was in eighth grade, she would talk about Frank Ocean with her friends from school.

He went to UNO, she would say. That's where I want to go.

He lives in LA, she would say. That's where I want to move to.

He has the best style range of anyone who's making music, now. Like, how he sings R&B, jazz, and raps. He also has the best abs.

Did you know that he's, like, gay? Her friends would say whenever she would talk about his abs.

He is bisexual, the older sister would correct her friends.

But for a guy, though, right, bisexual is gay.

The older sister always rolled her eyes at things like this.

You like, have no idea what words even mean.

•

As the sky darkens and the blue-tinged shadows swallow up the mountains, hundreds, thousands, maybe millions of low lamps begin to glow. They line the highway walls, embedded in the concrete so the road below becomes a long, gold, shining string of light.

The father looks at them and smiles at the well-lit road. The mother looks at them and smiles because they make her feel safe. The older sister looks at them and thinks about the dark car, moving through this line of light just like the black bar on her screen. The younger sister looks at them and tries to count as many as she can. She can't. She quickly loses track. She gets frustrated with the concept of the lights, the concept of a thing so numerous it can't be counted.

I'm hungry, says the younger sister.

No, you're not, the father says.

I know I am, she says. I'm hungry *now*.

The father sighs. He doesn't want to leave the highway's long, bright line, although he realizes that he too is hungry *now*. He glances at a sign of icons, pulls off at the exit. *In one mile, make a u-turn,* says the disapproving GPS.

They pull into a brown-brick, brown roof, diner-tavern restaurant. They file inside and seat themselves around a dim-lit, dark-wood booth. The waitress passes out a set of forks, knives, spoons, and thin red plastic cups covered with tiny hairline scratches.

The older sister orders first. A garden salad with no croutons. Oil, vinegar in cups, please, on the side.

The father groans. A salad?

I'm a vegetarian, she tells her father for the hundred thousandth time.

The younger sister has been staring at the pictures on the menu, most especially the spicy chicken sandwich. She is picturing a fire burning in her mouth, emitting smoke streams as she belches out a hot bright ball of flame. She thinks, tonight's the night when I will get the spicy chicken, and it's going to be extra fire-breathing spicy hot. But, what if it's *too* hot, she wonders, and I burn my tongue, or worse, burn holes inside my throat, and never swallow anything again? She pictures doctors reaching down into her throat with shiny tubes and knives to fill the burned-out, steaming holes so she can swallow.

What would you like? The waitress asks the younger sister.

Chicken—um—the chicken…nuggets, she says, and she swallows hard.

I'll have the portabella melt, the mother says. She hesitates, then adds, a glass of wine, please. Cabernet.

We don't have that, the waitress says. Just red.

The mother bites her lip. She makes a little hissing sound. Okay, that's fine.

The father contemplates the dinner-breakfast options and decides upon the special, something that they call the western skillet.

The waitress asks him, do you want to get smothered and covered?

The father contemplates what that might mean.

The mother looks at him like, no.

The father looks at her like, yes.

He says, yes, and the waitress takes their menus. She returns shortly with their food. The older sister sighs because her garden salad's covered in white dressing.

The younger sister bites a nugget, thinks, I'm such a coward, and the father starts to eat his smothered, covered western skillet. He pauses halfway through and makes a face. This thing is terrible.

The mother sips her wine and looks gently betrayed.

•

*I thought that I was dreaming,* Frank Ocean intones, again, after the car has passed innumerable lights and shadows. *I couldn't see you coming,* he laments as the triumphant GPS announces, *You have reached your destination.*

They park in front of their hotel room, which is on the upstairs rim of two, long rows that curve into an arch. The arch curls out onto a mostly empty parking lot, which leads out to the road that leads out to the beach.

The night is cool. The air is thick with salt, with sounds of insects, distant music, distant cars and ocean waves. The air is thick with strange sensations, strange, dark possibilities that hover in the sounds of the unseen.

The parents, tired from the road, sink down into the switching, flipping rhythms of the satellite remote control. The sisters ask if they can swim. They say, yes, in the pool, so they change into their new suits they picked out just for the trip.

The older sister takes her suit into the bathroom, where she folds each item of her clothing on a towel on the floor. She looks at her reflection in the dull hum of the light. Her long, blonde hair, bright yellow edges, frayed, split ends. Her face, a big, bored oval. Blisters on her feet. Mosquito bites across her legs, bright red beneath this light.

Her nipples, two sore spots of strangeness on her chest. She touches them, hesitantly, and the feeling makes her shiver.

•

The pool is divided in two sections. First—the shallow end—is set inside the building, blue electric water trimmed in pale, teal tile, surrounded by some waxy, potted plants, some awkwardly misshapen mini cacti.

The younger sister dips in, climbs out of the pool, leans over the cacti, fingers hovering above the needles, dripping, thinking, *sharp, sharp, pointy, sharp, sharp, pointy, sharp*. She leans in, breathes in, reaches out her finger. Touches it. It isn't sharp.

The second side—the outdoor pool—is set apart, divided by a gray glass wall that you can swim beneath. Outside, it's dark. The pool, an electric blue bowl, set in black, reflecting lines of white light, dancing veins.

The older sister swims beneath the glass partition. The water is much colder on the other side. She holds her nose between her fingers, holds her breath. She feels her chest expand with breath. She dives down to the bottom of the pool.

She crouches at the bottom of the pool for a moment, listens to vibrations of non-sounds around her. The non-sounds of the generators, humming in strange harmony. Electric whines, dimmed, thickened by the water's depth.

She hears a chiming sound.

Another chiming sound.

A silence, and another chiming sound.

A deep, electric shudder, and the generators soften to a hiss.

Another chime. Another chime. Another chime.

When she comes up for air, the chimes—a digital phone sound—ring clear. The air feels sharp. She sees a person sitting on the deck.

A vague, dark outline, blue-lit by the pool. Intermittent chimes.

A face. A silhouette. The bright rectangle of a phone.

A thin man. Young, or youngish. Older than her, but not old.

She dives back down into the pool, swims beneath the dark partition.

Back and forth between the warm, bright, indoor lighting and the cold, dark, dancing glow. She shivers with the suddenness of these transitions.

She swims back to the outdoor pool, to the pool's edge. She squints toward the man.

He looks up. He waves. Hi.

She waves back. Hi.

She glances downward, treading water. Glances, slowly, up.

His phone chimes and he chuckles, softly. He looks like he might be watching her.

She looks back down, then looks back up, again.

He's looking at his phone.

She pushes off the pool's edge with her mosquito-bitten legs.

She kicks hard, lets herself glide from one section to another, pushes back and forth, from warm to cold, from light to dark, while thinking:

        indoor                    outdoor
        indoor                    outdoor
        indoor                    outdoor
        indoor                    outdoor
        indoor                    outdoor
        indoor                    outdoor
        indoor                    outdoor

•

The older sister lies in bed with damp hair, turned toward the wall. Her friends are messaging her from their various locations.

    So bored, ☹ types Jena Thompson.

                                        Yeah, me too, she types.

    I touched a dolphin, 🐬 types Kate Myers.

                                        She types back, so cool.

She nods off to the flashing of the names and words up on her screen until she gets a message from her best friend, Marianne Lee.

    I met up with a guy, types Marianne Lee.

                              😮 What was he like? She types.

    He has tattoos.

    I want to get one now.

                                 She types, what did you do?

Just bedroom stuff, types Marianne Lee.

At the house show.

Was the band good? She types.

Marianne Lee types, ha, no.

😚, types Marianne Lee.

She types, 🖤 😊 😚

She clicks her phone screen off. Stares at the black screen.

Marianne Lee is always meeting up with guys. Marianne Lee is taller, thinner than her other friends. Marianne Lee wears black. Marianne Lee lives down her block. Marianne Lee lives in a big white stucco house with strange-shaped windows. Marianne Lee has tiny freckles near her eyes. Marianne Lee has sleek black hair that shines, like seals swimming.

She sets her phone down on the bedside table. She watches a mosquito dancing up the gray-black wall. Its little glints of wings, its little shiver movements—*bedroom stuff*—its shrivel of a stomach, filled with other peoples' blood.

•

The mother, meanwhile, stands out on the back porch, in the dark. She sips a glass of cabernet and looks into a row of trees. The trees are filled with insects. She can hear them, whispering within the branches, in a sort of quiet, creaking chorus.

A low drone—like an organ—interrupted—every now and then—by crackled chirps, and high-pitched, buzzing chimes. The branches of the trees quiver ethereally, eerily, like something that belongs beneath the ocean. She watches them and listens, through the hum of insects, for the distant ocean. Thinks about the ocean waves. She thinks about their darkness, gleaming vaguely. Of the water. Of the cold. About how cold the waves would be.

She thinks of drifting on them, drifting off, away from shore, of slipping…but a loud sound interrupts her thoughts.

The insect chorus swells into a sharp roar, for a moment.

Then, it dies.

Her throat stings.

She has swallowed too much wine.

•

Breakfast is poptarts—for the sisters—coffee—for the parents.

Swimming! Shouts the younger sister, pulling on her still-wet suit.

When I'm done with the paper, says the father without looking up.

The father takes forever finishing the paper.

Let's go back to the pool, says the older sister.

Sure, that's fine, the mother waves them on. She sits and sips her coffee. She makes sad little exhalations as the pages turn.

The older sister sighs. Come on, she murmurs. Let's just go.

The blue-green of the pool is not quite as clear amid the brightness of the sun. The water is much warmer. The transition from indoor to outdoor is not as sharp. The older sister shuts her eyes. She lets the two sides blur together.

Eventually, the thin young man returns. Alone. He's wearing dark blue swim shorts and a stretched out white t-shirt.

He waves. Hi.

She waves. Hi.

He takes the t-shirt off, sets it behind him.

She looks up at him. He looks okay.

He sits down on the pool's edge, dips half his legs in, kicks below the water, making shiny little waves.

I like the way you swim, he says.

Oh, thank you, says the older sister.

Like a seal, says the young thin man.

The older sister thinks of Marianne Lee, and she smiles. She is flattered by the indirect comparison. She dives back down, kicks off the edge, and power kicks between both sides, then pops her head back up, gasping, like, see?

The young thin man smiles back. She thinks, he's younger than I thought. She takes a longer look. His smile is nice, and body…he has nice-ish abs. He's not Frank Ocean, although he is likely not bisexual. Bisexual means that your body's perfect.

The younger sister crouches by the cactus, once again. She touches it. Still dull. Not sharp. She thinks, so disappointing. So, she pushes down, and down, until the point enters her skin.

A tiny drop of blood.

She winces.

She thinks, victory.

•

The family goes out for lunch. They choose a restaurant that overlooks the beach, with vinyl booths and picture windows. The father gets a burger and the mother gets a turkey burger and the older sister gets a fruit plate.

The younger sister gets the spicy chicken sandwich. *Yes*. This is the day. She looks at it and contemplates its color, peels back the bun, observes the white, coagulated mayo, drizzled full of red lines from the extra spicy sauce. She pats the bun back down. She holds the sandwich in her hands. She breathes in. Okay, I am ready, she thinks. She bites down. She closes her eyes for a moment to absorb the spiciness. Her moment never comes because the sandwich is not spicy.

They chew their food and watch the ferries leave the harbor, churning thin, white trails of froth that cut into the deep blue-gray. The seagulls hop among the broken stones and concrete slabs. They pick at bits of garbage, shrieking, flapping, for no reason.

•

The mother tells the older sister she is old enough to wander through the town. The father doesn't argue. So, she nibbles off the final fleck of watered honeydew and sets her plate aside, sets off to see what she can find.

She walks along the docks, looks at the bobbing boats, their female names. *Amelia. Kathleen O' Malley. Dulcinea. Dorothy, My Girl. Estella. Foxy Brown. Joanna. June Bug. Lorelai. Luna Lucille. Mary of the Sea. Goodbye, My Girl.*

She walks along the quiet streets filled with Victorian homes: tall, ornate-trimmed houses, shades of faded pastel paint. She passes by the numerous art galleries with crude ceramics, awkward charcoal life drawings, and crappy oil landscapes.

The sun grows hot as she reaches the town's main square. She comes against a sudden burst of people from the downtown farmer's market. She weaves her way through sandaled feet, through bodies wearing different shades of linen, bearing tote bags filled with vegetables.

She brushes up against a table filled with fresh-picked blackberries. She takes one from the box and pops it in her mouth.

She finds a table filled with tasting samples from a winery. She sneaks a plastic cup and downs it in one gulp.

She takes a free fan from a local politician's booth and waves toward her, with the blank side pointing out, the text side pointing in. The paper fan wafts his name in her face, repeatedly. The fan goes: *swish swish, Gerry Gerrish, Gerry Gerrish.*

She sees a girl that looks like Marianne Lee, and another girl that looks like Marianne Lee with short hair, and yet another girl that looks like Marianne Lee with blue dyed hair and a rather striking, very nearly see-through sea-green dress.

•

The mother and the father and the younger sister move down to the beach. They walk along the water, toting canvas bags. The younger sister skitters out into the waves, then back. Look what I found. Her footprints form a zig-zag pattern in the sand.

She holds her hand out for the mother.

Look.

Two shards of beach glass, smoothed and rounded by the tide, frosted with salt and sand.

Look.

Seven ordinary bleached shells—two half-shattered—otherwise, the same.

Nice, says the mother.

When the younger sister's back is turned, she pitches them away.

The younger sister grinds her feet into the big green balls of kelp, delighted and repulsed as they deflate with hissing pops of air. The dark, translucent stalks around them look like strands of hair from some strange monster, from some witch that lives within the sea.

They come into a long and empty stretch of beach, divided in two parts. The first: a pebbled outer layer, trimmed with blonde grass, large, gray mounds of driftwood, gnarled roots of washed-up trees. The second: flat sand. Here, the mother spreads a blanket, opens up the canvas bags.

The mother and the father open up a six-pack, sit, and read. The mother reads a book. The father reads the paper.

Still the paper? Says the mother.

A light breeze ruffles its pages. It's important not to lose track of what's going on.

The younger sister wanders through the beach. She watches how the sand appears to come alive beneath her feet. The small crabs scurry. Waves lap at the shore as thousands of small holes gasp open to absorb the waves, like many thirsty mouths.

Sometimes, she sees a palm-sized jellyfish, a flat, blue, dried-up disc, an under-body splayed with skinny ciliated threads. The dried blue disc is topped off with a clear, half-circle sail. They look so delicate, she thinks, like mini spaceships made of glass.

She wades into the water, lunges face-first into waves. She sputters salt, spits. Lunges. Sputters. Salt goes up her nose.

She lets herself drift with the tide.

Looks at the beach, back at her parents.

They are little speck-dolls, sinking in the sand.

She watches as their movements become hazier and hazier, like figures in slow-motion on a distant screen.

Saltwater drizzles down her face, gets in her eyes, and blurs them, as they grow smaller and smaller, as she drifts further away.

•

That night, the older sister lies in bed, listening to Frank Ocean sing about a certain kind of love and loss. He sings, *your dilated eyes.* He sings the pale sky, *watch the clouds float.*

*White Ferrari.*

*White Ferrari.*

*White Ferrari.*

She thinks about the many different versions of Marianne Lee, all living in a white room in her head. A blank white box filled with Marianne Lees, sitting and standing, talking to each other, dressing each other, and undressing each other.

She thinks about the blue haired Marianne Lee and the see-through sea-green dress. She peers into the white room of her thoughts. She thinks about the sea-green dress. She starts to peer a little closer…

Thinks about Frank Ocean.

Thinks about Frank Ocean's abs.

She thinks:

Green dress

Green buttons, unbuttoning

Green straps, falling

Pale skin, pink nipple

Pale skin amid dark tufts of hair

Pale skin amid the *White Ferrari*

Pale counters of her *White Ferrari*

Pale edges of her *White Ferrari*

*White Ferrari*

She listens to the song, until the black bar has filled in.

She clicks her phone off and she stares into the blank screen.

She tries to fall asleep, but she can't sleep.

She turns her phone back on.

She types to Marianne Lee, there's a cute guy here.

• 

The next morning, the older sister walks along the docks, along the pathway she has carved out in her mind. She thinks, *hello, Amelia, hello, Kathleen O' Malley, hello, Dulcinea, hello, Dorothy, My Girl.*

She passes by the pastel houses and the galleries, looks vaguely into windows, into curtains shifting.

A cat sits in a window, yowling at nobody in particular.

A plastic bag skates, softly, through the street.

She comes into the town square, and she sees the thin young man. He's walking parallel to her, across the street. He waves and walks toward her. She keeps walking in the same direction.

Hi, he says, behind her.

Right behind her.

She turns. Hi.

They walk in silence for awhile, pointing every now and then at things they can both see. Haha, a yowling cat.

Haha, a dick tag on a brick wall.

Haha, look at that guy's face, up on that sign.

It's Gerry Gerrish. He is bald and long-faced. She feels bad for him.

My name is LJ, says the young thin man.

She says, hi, LJ.

I'm so hungry, LJ says. Have you had breakfast?

She says, no.

Let's go get breakfast, says LJ, and they walk together, back the way she came, to reach the restaurant along the docks.

They sit across from one another in the booth behind the one her family sat inside, the day before. The booth is empty now, but she keeps glancing at it, over LJ's shoulder, like she half expects to see them.

What's up? He asks her.

Nothing. Sorry. She orders the fruit plate and a coffee that she doesn't really drink.

He gets a skillet—extra sausage, extra gravy—smiles as she nibbles at a rind of cantalope. You like fruit, huh?

She shrugs. I am a vegetarian.

He says, that's cool. I think about things like that, sometimes. He takes a bite of sausage. He smiles as he swallows. He does have a nice smile. Big, white teeth.

She smiles back at him with a closed mouth.

They talk about the town—he lives nearby—the mountains—where he used to live—the restaurant—he used to work in a place like this—family—two brothers, older than him—family trips—they suck—his favorite color, gray blue, like a stormy sky.

Me too, she says. She's just now realized this fact about herself.

Everything is gray blue here, he says. It's a good place to be, if that's your thing.

They laugh, as if this town were nothing but a gray blue brush of paint.

He pays for both of them.

She thanks him.

I guess we'll just walk back together, since we're at the same place, he says.

She says, I think I might want to walk a bit, by myself.

If that's what you want, he says. He leans down, hovers for a moment, then he leans in close to kiss her on the mouth.

The kiss tastes bad—like sausage—and his teeth feel really big. They butt around and scrape and click against her own. His tongue pokes at her teeth, insistently, until she opens them. She lets his tongue lick at her tongue, which lays there, flat, unsure.

I'll see you later, then, he smiles when the kiss is over, takes her number, puts his number in her phone.

Mhm. Later, she says. Her voice is breathy, like a little kid's.

She thinks, that's not her real voice.

She sounds so dumb and wrong.

•

Back at the hotel, everyone is on a different screen. Her mother and her younger sister tap their tablets. Her father's looking at the weather on the Weather Channel, echoing the forecast out loud. Sunny. Chance of showers. Rain.

The morning passes into afternoon, this way, until the rain begins to fall.

The father says, goddamn the Weather Channel.

The rain begins to fall hard, hissing as it hits the ground.

The mother moves out to the porch and pours a glass of wine.

•

The older sister gets a message from LJ:

☺ Hi

                                    She types, hi. ☺

He types, ☁

                                  She types, yeah, it sucks.

He types, the color though.

                                  She types, haha.

He types, I want to see you soon.

                                  She types, later maybe.

He types, 😚

And a little later, he types, 😚

She looks into the screen. She starts to type, then stops.

She turns the screen off. Looks up at the blank white of the ceiling.

She thinks, I don't know what to think.

She thinks, don't think.

She tries hard not to think, and feels a satisfying sickness in her stomach.

•

A few more days go by like this, the television glowing, tablets on. Every now and then, a message coming in.

The younger sister yawns.

The older sister shifts around, not thinking, watching couples argue about houses on

HG TV.

I'm never getting married, says the younger sister.

Like you're old enough to know, the older sister says.

The couples choose between their top three houses, all of which are flawed, and none of which they seem to like that much.

•

At a sleepover last summer, all the older sister's friends were talking about famous people that they liked. They started off comparing famous women to themselves—she's kind of fat—I want her hair—you're prettier than her.

She has nice legs, the older sister said.

Her friends gave her a look.

I mean, she does!

Marianne Lee laugh-coughed, then. Lesbo.

I mean, I'm jealous of them, she corrected herself.

Don't be jealous—you look great, her friends all reassured her.

They talked about the boys they liked—both famous and non-famous—and they asked the older sister who she'd choose.

Frank Ocean, she decided. The first name that came to mind.

Her friends approved her choice, with varying degrees of hesitancy.

•

I'm old enough to know, the younger sister says. It's not like you know anything.

The older sister nods.

The couples finish arguing, then choose the least offensive choice, then they pretend to be excited on TV.

This show's depressing, says the older sister.

This show's funny, says the younger sister. Everybody's dumb.

I guess that's funny, if you think you're smart, the older sister says.

The older sister doesn't think she's smart.

Meanwhile, the rain keeps raining, running down the glass, still tapping at that strange sensation in her stomach, stirring drifts of fog. The gray blue sky remains—her newly chosen favorite shade—reminding her of him whenever she looks out the window.

•

Meanwhile, the mother stands and stares out at the rain.

She sips her glass of wine until it's finished, pours another splash.

The father comes behind her, puts his arms around her waist.

He murmurs, hey. His voice: that gentle, cautious voice she really hates.

He murmurs, lately you have been…I mean…think of your brother.

She does think of him. The rain. The darkness of the sky. She sighs. She looks up and she finishes her wine. She looks directly at the father, reaches for the bottle, and pours more.

•

The rain stops, and the white sun seems to burn away the lost time.

They go to the beach. This time, the older sister joins them.

She shows a little kid how to build castles out of dripping sand. You get it wet, then let it drizzle down, like this.

The little kid refuses to be bothered with the subtleties of dripping into fine points, into fine accumulations.

It's a blob! He screams. He slams his fists into the castle, runs away.

The older sister shakes her head and scoops a new handful of sand.

She crouches down above the frothy damp line where the waves keep breaking, gets the sand wet, sits, and drizzles down a new foundation.

Kids don't get how to do kid things, she thinks. Ultimately, no one really understands the way to be the way they are.

The younger sister sees another jellyfish.

Another, and another.

Suddenly, she sees a clearing where the tide gets caught, with dozens, maybe hundreds of their tiny, blue disc bodies.

She thinks, wow.

She thinks, oh shit.

She thinks, amazing.

She stands above a still wet, not yet dried up jellyfish.

She takes a piece of driftwood, pokes at it, and steps away.

She steps up, swiftly jabs the stick into its body, skewers it, and stands, and stares.

The jellyfish does nothing.

•

They go back to the restaurant. The father gets a turkey burger, looks up at the mother, who smiles, lightly. The mother orders French silk pie, and nothing else. The older sister gets a side of French fries with her fruit plate.

The younger sister gets the spicy chicken sandwich, asks for extra hot sauce, thinking, let's try this again. She takes a bite, and oh it burns, it burns, it burns! She downs a glass of water, gasping. She thinks, victory.

The older sister makes it halfway through her fries before she gets a message from LJ: *I'll meet you there at 9.* She asks the younger sister if she wants the rest of her fries.

Obviously, yeah. The younger sister takes her plate and eats them.

The mother smiles at this act of sharing. You're so sweet. The mother kisses her forehead, kisses her cheek.

The older sister smiles queasily. Her mother smells like wine. Hey, how's your pie?

The mother shrugs. Okay.

•

It's 8:51 when she makes it to the docks. The sun is just beginning to go down. She paces, looking at the boats. Some names are gone, replaced by others. *Don Juan*, *Heat Wave*, *Paradise*, *Obsession*, *Happy and Alone*.

She sees the dark speck of his form approaching at 9:10. She walks toward the dark speck. Lets him take her in his arms.

He smells like mints, this time.

He whispers, hey.

She whispers, hey.

He kisses her cheek.

She kisses his cheek.

It tastes like lotion.

You smell good, he says.

They walk along the beach. They watch the sun burn bright. Reflected streaks—like cinders—dance impossibly along the waves.

The streaks dim down to violet, replaced by bobbing, far-off lights. She smiles at them. She thinks, that's what the boats became.

The air is thick with salt, with sounds of insects, distant music from the boats. A dull thrum, punctuated by some *yeahs*, and *woos*. He takes her hand. He leads her to a shadowed inlet where the air is cooler, with a stronger, fishy water smell.

I thought that I was dreaming when I saw you, he says.

*Yeah, woo!* Shout the boats.

I never could've seen it coming.

He gives her a mint kiss. This time, she tells her tongue to move. It does. He moves his hands down to her back, down lower, lower. *Woo*.

She hears a clinking sound, a swishing sound, a zipping sound. A gentle cough. A shifting, and a deeper cough. Mhm. Another kiss. She doesn't move her tongue, this time. He takes her hands and moves them to his waist. Then lower, lower.

Hey...she says.

He whispers, it's okay.

It feels strangely warm, yet frozen, like a limb your nerves have not yet reached, an anxious, straining, but not yet sensitive part.

He moans. He feels what she's doing—even if she doesn't—as she realizes that her hand is clasped and stroking.

It is a smooth, yet ridged thing. A muscle, moving. She can feel it getting thicker, warmer, and this makes her concentrate. *Okay.* There is a bad smell. It is probably the fish water. A bad sensation, in her stomach. That is not his fault.

She thinks
smoothridged
frozenwarm
mintsausage
breathingbreathing
bad smellgood smell
bad sensationgood sensation
bad sensationgood sensation
breathingbreathing
breathinghard breath
hard breath good
hard musclegood
hard motiongood
hard moaninggood
hard hard hard hard…
hard hard hard hard ………
hard hard hard hard……………
hard hard hard hardgood good good good good
good good good good
good good good
good good
good good
good
He says, are you okay?
She says, um, yeah.
He says, um…
She is shaking.
Look, he says, if you're not into this…
She thinks, fuck fuck fuck *fuck*…

They sit together, for awhile, staring at the boat lights, getting cold, the night wind blowing hard, the salt air stinging.

He says, it's okay.

She says, no…

It's okay…

*No*, it's *not* okay.

He stays there, sitting with her, but he shifts, a bit, away.

Although her heart is shuddering, her shoulders shivering, she feels like she's floating, somewhere, out of body, in the dark.

She thinks, I'm sorry.

Says, I'm so sorry.

He laughs, drily. Don't be.

Is she sorry?

She feels sorry.

She knows she feels something.

I am gonna go, he says.

She says, all right. It comes out in the airy child's voice, the voice that isn't hers.

She wonders what is really hers.

She thinks, I don't know, and she tries to turn the thought into, I don't care, but she can't.

She thinks, I don't know anything.

I'm bad at being anything.

I'm bad at being anyone.

I'm bad at being real.

•

I met up with a guy, she types to Marianne Lee.

Where? Types Marianne Lee.

She types, by the beach 🛥️ 🦀 🗿

Marianne Lee types, 😍

What was it like?

            She types, 🙂

Marianne Lee types, that's so cool.

I have always wanted to meet someone by
the beach.

For just a moment, she feels warmed by this attention,

until Marianne Lee types: I'm so jealous! ;
😌🤏😌

         She types back, don't be jealous.
         Starts to type, it wasn't even good.
           Instead, she types back, 🖤

Marianne Lee types, 🖤

•

The next morning, the older sister stays in bed with headphones on, listening to Frank Ocean singing *White Ferrari*.
 She imagines white rooms filled with women—filled with Marianne Lees—fading into outlines, into ghost shapes, into nothing.
*Bad luck to talk on these rides*
*Mind on the road, your dilated eyes*
She thinks about the long ride—home—ahead of them.
She thinks about a big house, filled with white rooms.
*White Ferrari*
Thinks of white clouds, drifting, fading.
*Had a good time.*

•

The family goes back—one last time—to the beach. The mother and the father sit together as he reads the news. He passes her each section as he finishes. The sun is warm, but mild, and the sky is blue. It is a very nice day.

The younger sister walks along the water, picking up pieces of stones and broken shells and broken glass. She carries them with her until she has too much to hold, and then she pitches them—one by one—back into the waves.

She smashes her bare heels into the kelp bubbles and bursts them in a violent, stomping, popping, hissing trail, almost steps onto a jellyfish. Her bare toe barely grazes it. She feels its jellied skin, steps back, and shudders from the feeling.

She wades into the water, walks into the waves until they reach her neck. She kicks out, paddles deeper, farther from the shore. She sees the speed boats in the dark blue water, churning thick, white foam, the line of buoys separating beach from open sea.

She paddles out, up to the line. She grabs hold of a buoy, bobs there, looking at the great, big, blue immensity.

She hangs on, for a moment, waiting for something to happen. Nothing does.

She lets herself slip down, beneath the boundary.

# SOLITAIRE

A lover—who is not a friend—emails me, one morning—as he often does—to give instructions for my day. He tells me what to eat and what to wear, the way to bathe (or, not to bathe,) how many times I should (or should not) masturbate. I've come to see this lover as a strange image consultant who instructs me in the art of making bad decisions. He tells me of his plan—to make me meet a man, to make him pay to meet me—in a set of emails titled *Whore*.

This set of emails opens: *Sex for money. Sacrificial kindness. Two conflicting images—conflicting when applied to you?*

Three emails later, he writes: *Sunset Hotel.*

Seven later: *Two thousand, in cash.*

Eight later: *Better make a list.*

I call him, anxious to discuss his plan. Of course, he doesn't answer.

He is teasing me, ignoring me again.

I pad into the bathroom, sigh. Peel off my shirt, my loose pants, and my leg brace. Take a last look at my naked nails.

•

Here I am—then—a woman most would probably describe as young, crouched on the bathroom floor, in basic black lace lingerie. This is to say: one of two bras I own, one of two thongs. This one I'm wearing—here—was stolen just for such occasions.

My hair: short, black. Specifically, a blunt dyed bob with square-cut bangs. My real hair, though everyone assumes it is a wig. Painting my nails, wearing glasses I don't usually wear, preferring things I see to be a little blurry.

•

Painting my nails forces me to see the scars across my hands, which I received working the day shift at a group home for clients with special needs. One of my client's special needs was touch. He tried to hold my hand, and when I brushed him off, he dug his nails in deep.

I took that job because I needed work, but it fulfilled some other needs that I could never quite seem to explain. There's really no good way to reconcile a one-time *yes* with the reality of waking every day at 4:30 am. This work appealed to something in me, I suppose. Walking out to my car, in darkness. Strange, sick energy I seemed to store inside my lungs, then breathe in cold, deep breaths while pacing down the hall, keys clinking, thinking, this is mine, this energy belongs to me.

Picture me, folding towels, clothes with labeled names, darting through hallways, doors. Please take my word that I was very good at this. I thrived on little food and sleep, despite the tempting smells of sizzled hash browns, buttered toast I took the time to make just right.

The sounds of bed sheets shifting, tired whines. Their poor, soft eyes. Flushed faces, gummy mouths, limbs slick with piss. Me whispering, good morning. Kneeling down low, as I always did, to help them into wheelchairs, despite the sharp pains stirring in my legs.

I was already pushing my boundaries and letting them be pushed. When I was hired there, I said I would not drive the old 16-passenger van. But within the first week, I was called to fill in for a different shift, felt guilty, said yes, drove the van that night, white knuckled down the highway.

•

But I no longer work that job. I had to quit because my left leg fell asleep, one day, refused to wake back up. More to the point: my left leg fell asleep amidst a bondage game. My back was tied up to a pole, my ankles tied up to my legs.

The lover walked away, pretended to ignore me, then pretended I was just pretending when I cried out from some shooting pain.

You should've told me, he said, later, when he helped me, limping, to his car. I cannot help you if you cannot tell me what you need.

•

I make a list entitled, WHAT I WILL NOT DO. It reads:
    no alcohol
    no knives
    no unprotected sex
    no large, visible bruises
    no marks on my face, of any kind
    no vocal restrictions (gags)
    no photographs
    no leaving me alone
    no anal sex

•

Here I am—now—a woman some would probably describe as young, if they weren't looking very closely at my face. Crouched on my bed, wearing a long black slip, with pillows propped behind my neck. Imagining myself—as I was—then.

My hair: long, red. Not dyed: embellished. That is what I say, though no one cares. Yes, it is natural. It is my real hair.

My reading glasses, which I need to wear more often, now, although I still prefer the way the world looks without them.

•

The red paint drools down between the cracks, between the nails and the skin, between the outsides and the insides of my hand. I soak the swabs in alcohol. I wipe the edges, scrape the insides of the edges of my fingers with a metal file.

I fail at these kinds of things. I always have. The lover said, though, that he likes red nails, so I have to try.

My nails look like shit.
So, I redo them.
And redo them.

And redo them.
And redo them.
They still look like shit.

•

Recently, I've devoted myself to the art of developing boring addictions. My current addiction is online Solitaire. I sit and click the cards into correct piles. Soothing. Gambling with no stakes, wherein nothing can be lost.

The are four different card groups in Solitaire:

1. The Tableau—the main table of cards
2. The Foundations—four piles on which a whole sequence or suit must be built
3. The Stock (or Hand) Pile—where remaining cards accumulate
4. The Talon (or Waste) Pile—for cards that serve no purpose in The Tableau

That's where most of my cards end up, because I'm not especially attentive when I'm clicking at the screen.

A four of hearts, a three of spades, a nine of diamonds, ten of clubs. Click, click. A jack of hearts. Click. Queen of spades. Click. And an ace. I bite my lip.

My husband comes behind me, gently gestures, doesn't that go there?

He doesn't understand the function of this game.

•

I arrive in a cab, in a black wrap dress, bent over crutches (the leg brace would snag on my stockings.) He waves from the front table, already sipping his scotch. He doesn't look as bad as I expected him to look, considering the lover told me he has cancer. His eyes look tired—gray-rimmed—not moreso than mine. His shaved head suits him, signifies his age more than his illness. I feel oddly disappointed by this man's apparent health, in contrast to the lover's dark descriptions.

He stands to greet me in an awkward shifting dance around my crutches, takes them from my arm, and sets them up against the wall.

A short peck on both cheeks. He smells like rich cologne. He sits back down.

He wears a turtleneck that makes my black wrap dress look cheap.

His voice is fast and loud and filled with emptiness, like: two blocks down on Sacramento, there's another strip joint, but in this one, they make girls wear nude-toned stockings, for hygienic reasons, probably, less fun though, peeking at their parts, through barriers like that.

I nod.

I trace the fork around along my plate. I dig the prongs in vein-like patterns through my rice. He's telling me about the history of Sicily, how it has been invaded many, many times.

A certain distrust, he says. In my blood.

I nod.

He laughs.

I turn back to my rice. He starts to talk about his wife.

Three years, no sex, he says.

A long time, I commiserate.

He says, it was, it was. He takes a hard sip of his scotch.

I add a little pepper to my rice. I take a bite. Still bland. I add a little more. I can't seem to taste anything.

I told her to put out, or get out, he explains to me.

Did she put out, or get out? I ask, and I take another bite.

Not either, he says. We have an arrangement. But, no trust.

The pepper tingles in my throat. I used too much.

I nod into my rice. I understand. Like Sicily.

He laughs. You make connections, he exclaims. He shakes his head.

You make connections, he repeats. I like that. Yeah, like Sicily. You make connections. You're not just a pretty face.

He's fat. I wouldn't mind the fat, just in and of itself, but he is such an odd fat, an unsettling arrangement of his flesh, the fat of someone who was thin, then fat, now strangely thin-fat, in a pale, pock-marked skin that sags like draining.

    He says, six months to live, they said.

    I nod.

    Six months ago, he laughs.

    I look back down. I do not know how to respond.

    Could go at any time. He plugs his laughter with a bite of veal.

    Chewing, chewing, chewing, chewing, chewing.

•

Click, click, click, click. My husband catches me, now, in the midst of my addiction. Kisses my cheek. Kisses my neck. Kisses my mouth. Gathers my hair, pulls at it a bit, the way he knows I like him to. Reaches behind my back and gently shuts the screen.

•

At the hotel, he gestures for me to walk on ahead of him. He mimes the movements of my legs with fingers in the air. It's almost funny, how his flitting joints bear so little resemblance to my stiff-limbed, crutch-supported real movement.

    Crutch comes down. Right foot. Left foot. Drag.

    Crutch comes down. Right foot. Left foot. Drag.

    Crutch comes down. Right foot—He lifts my skirt up from behind, left side, and I am almost grateful that it goes so smoothly, that my legs are objects that he actually wants to look at.

    He checks to see that I have worn the stockings.

    Garter belt, he murmurs. *Classy*, drawing out the *a* out in an impression of my voice. I say, I never liked that word. It's like some code. What does it mean?

    He says, it means you know what you are doing.

•

Inside the room, the door shuts, shoves me up against the mirror, and he grabs my shoulders, crutches, which go clattering somewhere into a corner, now out of my reach, pinches my tender points, nails hit a nerve, instantly, and I start to slip. He's practiced this.

He clicks the metal cuffs around my wrists.

He announces that he thinks I need a glass of wine.

He pours a glass. I shake my head, no, but he presses two firm fingers to my jaw, plying my teeth to open, pours into my mouth.

I swallow, shocked. I don't know what to do, now, and my instinct tells me, thank him, and so I sputter-mumble, thank you.

He tells me I am welcome, sets the wine glass down, and he gestures, sit. I sit down on the bed. He pulls a black strap from a drawer.

It is a reddish rubber ball. A gag.

I shake my head like, nonono.

Six months, he says.

I swallow. He is fat.

He kneels down—so he looks small as possible—beside the bed.

His pose reminds me of myself—knelt down to help my clients in their chairs—triggers a surge of strange cold energy, the kind of energy I've tried to feel again, re-feel, with the lover: the desire to be an instrument of use.

His rich perfume, now tinged with sweat, smells sad, grandfatherly. His eyes look darker, now. His shaved head, too—dry skin, greenish, ungleaming—from above him, looking down. I wonder if he knows this, but it doesn't really matter. I'm excited, sick with bright chill.

I part my mouth as though to speak, but I say nothing. Leaning in, I let him wrap the gag around me. Let him strap it on.

•

Knelt down before that now familiar smell of his engorged cock, mingled with my drizzled spit, my hands cupped underneath to catch the drips, the tip slid through my lips, then down my tongue, then down my throat, my now familiar reflexes producing just the right amount of bile.

 My husband strokes my hair.
 I murmur, to remind him, and he pulls it, harder.
 Gurgling, I thank him with a deep thrust to my throat.
 He thanks me with a moan, another, even deeper thrust.
 I almost gag. The chill runs through my veins.
 He murmurs, yes.
 Good girl.

•

A blindfold then appears, as he leans me back down into the bed. The feeling of a long, cold metal rod he ties between my legs.

 He's careful with the left leg, ties it looser. Does that feel okay? He asks.
 I mumble something like, mhm.
 The feeling of the ties, undone, around my waist, unwrapping of my wrap dress, pushing down my bra. I hear the sound of fabric shifting, bedsprings, and a dry inhale, exhale. Sound of sucking on my breasts.
 The feeling of his flesh, sagging and soft, pressed up against me.
 I think, I am glad that I cannot see what this looks like.
 I hear a new sound: click, click, click. The snapping of a camera.
 No, I think. I told him *no*. I told him—no—*specifically*.
 I try to tell him no, but what comes out just sounds like muffled spit, like someone else's muffled spit, like someone else's stupid moans.

•

When he has finished taking pictures, I hear something snip. Another snip. The soft flesh sliding off my bra, my thong. I think, now, hazily, I guess I'm down to just one bra, one thong, and not my nice ones. It's a good thing he is giving me two thousand dollars.

 I hear another, different click. A whir. He parts my legs. He strokes his fingers—wet, licked—slowly up and down my lower lips, pressing the vibrator against my clit, until I start to feel my muscles urge themselves—against my will—to just relax.

I feel his cock tap up against my inner thigh. It feels long, but thin—still half soft, hardening with each tap, tap, tap, tap. It feels strangely curved, and stranger, when he enters me. I realize—alarmed, at first, then absently—he's not wearing a condom.

My mind flits all around my body, trying to detect sensation from the surfaces I cannot see. My wrists begin to tingle. Then, the tingle fades, and then, my wrists, my hands, begin to feel detached from me.

I think about the soup I made for lunch today. The last can. Green pea-something, with its sad smell, like a nursing home. I do not like that flavor, but I told myself I wouldn't let it go to waste, that someone had to eat it.

The turning of my wrist—now cuffed—to slice around the rim. Then, peel back the lid, the jagged teeth—the mouth—of a tin can. The scraping of a spoon. The sipping of a mouth—now gagged. The swallowing. The smell. I think, what was I thinking?

•

And…
 For a moment: silence.
 For another moment: silence.
 For another: silence.
 And another, and another: silence.
 Then, his laughter, from across the room.
 A soft laugh, meant for someone else.
 A phone laugh, words projecting, softly, so far from this room.
*A letto*, I hear him whisper, in a voice I have not heard him use, into the other voice behind the phone.
 *Magari fosse così. Forse.*
 *Caro, caro. Sì.*
 *Se mi dici che lo vuoi così*. He laughs a light laugh.
 *Ok. Ok. Bene. Se lo dici tu.*

•

Meanwhile, there's a soft glow I can sense, still, through the blindfold. From the lamp, off to the right, above the bedside table.

I imagine that the softness of his voice is somehow tied into the softness of the light, like something in it will protect me.

I lie there, reaching through the room through my imagination, which is dumbly blurred, but soft, protective, like the light. The phone…was on the table, by the lamp. My crutches…No, the counter, by the TV. No, the other table…No…it doesn't matter.

I start to count, inside my head, two thousand dollars. What it will—and will not—do for me, and what it will—and will not—buy. Two months of rent. Two months of food. Two months of jobless time, for planning, thinking, and I think, two thousand dollars isn't much.

I think, six months, six months.

I feel pity for this man.

I want to feel pity for him.

I want to be kind.

His gentle voice keeps whispering these words I do not know, and I know then that I am not there for the money.

•

What am I—was I—here for—there for?

I still do not know.

I never did.

How could I—then—if I do not know—now?

I just sit, hand on head, my fingers kneading at the strands of hair, as though I might extract some essence from their roots.

•

Meanwhile, I should mention that the gag fills up my mouth, leaving no space for all the liquid that belongs in there, and thus, a thin spit stream begins to flow, begins to build in viscousness, until it forms a thick wet pool around my face.

•

I focus on the glow, letting my thoughts go slack in repetitions of the obvious/non-obvious, like *it will be okay*, when I don't know if *it* will, or what *it* might even be, but it will *be*, okay, it will *all*, *be*, *okay*.

    I focus on the glow, while drifting in and out of what I only dimly understand as consciousness.

    The glow dies and the phone clicks into its receiver.

    The light behind the blindfold flickers out.

•

He grabs my arms my shoulders neck my hair twist flip flap face slap back spine crack spit slime fat ass fat face fat hand the smell of fat spread sweat slap face slap slap slap spit slap kissing kissing kiss then spit slap face back spine then hand then neck then hand then hand around my neck now choking choking choking clogged nose clogged up sticking sticking stuck now stuck now so so so cannot breathe I cannot cannot cannot breathe I breathe scream he stuffs a wad a sock a stocking in my mouth my spit smell foot stain tasting sour drizzle flecking choking harder harder cannot cannot really really cannot fucking breathe I scream I scream shh shh shh shh shhshhhhhhhhhh-shut-the-fuck-up-shut-the-FUCK-UP whispering no hissing now no not the caro-caro whispering the hissing pig-shit-bitch he hisses pig-shit-whore my eyes hurt drooling drooling look-at-what-you-did-bitch but I obviously can't spit-sick-drip-drenching I will take his word for it he pulls my hair back pushes up my ass and nonononono I told him *NO* specifically and no and *no* and yes and yes he does he shoves his cock inside my ass my ass my legs limp finger on my clit slick with my spit he rubs around that is the worst this spit drenched finger now two fingers kneading deeper in now deeper in so spit slick a new skin a numbing numbing thud still deeper kneading in this inlet spittle seeping deeper deeper I say to myself get in get in get in get in before he can.

•

Some tiny little actress comes and takes my place.
    She moves around from under then, on top, upon the bed.
    She makes him come.
    She gets into the shower.
    Wraps her arms around his knees.
    Please.
    Puts his hand upon her head.
    Thank you.
    She speaks no more.
    She stares.
    Up.
    At his cock.
    The limp.
    Clay brown.
    The soft.
    Drained.
    Organ.
    Bloodless.
    Wet, clean.
    Warm.
    Steam.
    Fogging.
    Smell, hot skin.
    Salt, sags of warmth.
    And puckers, pimples.
    Webs and webs and webs.
    Of thick wet hair.
    Steam, thick. Warm.
    Fogging, fogging,
    fogging, fogging,

  fogging
  fogging
  fogging.

•

Here I am—now—again.

  Click, click. The jack, onto the queen, onto the king. Click. Queen on king. Click.

  Missed something, again. No going back. New game.

  My husband comes behind me. Kisses. Gathers up my hair. Whispers, and pulls me from my world. Shuts the screen.

•

Here I am—was—then.

  Reading emails that the lover sent: a set entitled *Cara Mia* following the set entitled *Whore*.

  He thinks it's best for him if he no longer sees or speaks to me. He says, *you've never told me, no. I worry that you don't know how.*

•

I stay with him that night because he asks me to.

  I lie awake. My hair lies wet around me on the bed.

  I lie awake and wet and cold until it dries, at last, and then I slip into a sleep in which I dream of nothing.

•

I get into the cab he calls. I give the driver my address. The driver seems confused by my directions. I have no confidence in my ability to speak. So, I just gesture, vaguely. That way. Just go that way. For awhile.

  I open up my purse. I try to count my money. With each set of hundred bills I touch, I bite down, lightly, on my lip.

Ten. Twenty. Thirty. Fifty. One hundred. I bite down.
Twenty. Forty. Fifty. Seventy. Ninety. Two Hundred. I bite down.
I count two thousand.
Try to tuck it in an envelope.
The envelope bursts open, so I lick it.
Seal it.
Bite down hard.
The driver circles round my neighborhood.
I sit there, staring out the window, like I don't know where I am.
I watch the numbers add up on the counter in the cab.
The driver just drives on.
He thinks that I am high, or drunk, or something.
I allow him to keep driving.
Thinking.
Dumbly.
Maybe.
Somehow.
If the numbers just add high enough…
Something will change…
That we…
Will shine our headlights.
Into some gray land of dim, forever mornings.
Where I've never said yes.
Thank you.
No.
To anyone.

IV

# THE WIDOWER

The old man knows he is—or was—at one point—married. He remembers traces of their marriage, reoccurring moments.

Pink sunlight through the curtains of their kitchen.

Sipping coffee.

Gray-blue moonlight through the curtains of their bedroom.

Getting into bed.

Above all, he recalls her shape—the imprint of her shape—the space she occupied in bed, the mark that she was there.

He can remember what she smelled like, though he cannot name it, but sometimes he catches a reminder in something he passes by.

A breath of fresh-cut flowers.

Open windows.

Dew from recent rain.

Tea leaves dipped down into the steam he stirs.

The ghostly trails they leave.

He can't remember what her face looked like, though sometimes he recalls her mouth, her nose, her eyes, but always individually. Not a face, but features floating on some pale tide of recognition. When he stirs them, they drift down to darkness, out of reach.

•

He squints into the pink light and he turns in bed. A thin twin, for one person. Cold. He coughs. He reaches for his watch. He puts it on. It feels hard against the raised vein of his wrist. He coughs. He eases slowly toward the edges of his bed.

He slips his feet into his slippers, ties his robe. Rough terry. Tender skin.

He pads into the bathroom. Stands before the sink. He puckers at the gray-white face. He lets the water run over his hands. The skin is loose. Ripples of mounds, like hills of wax. He shakes the hills until they're dry depressions, dries them, reaches for the glass that holds the teeth.

He looks into the tumbler at the teeth. A cloudy puddle, gray against the pink, a pool in its gums.

He shakes the teeth. They clatter, softly, in his hand. He puts them in his mouth. He shifts his lips against their slick, tart, strangeness.

He makes a frail stream of piss.

Steam rises and he thinks of tea.

He thinks of coffee.

Thinks about his wife.

Tries to imagine her.

Tries to imagine morning, with her.

Coffee. Tea.

Steam fades.

A tinge of pain.

He thinks, he can't.

He flushes.

•

He glances at his calendar. It's Wednesday. Laundry morning. So, he shuffles to the bed. He peels back the pastel sheets. He thinks they look like something that a woman would pick out. He can't remember purchasing or picking out these sheets.

He bundles them into a ball. He holds the ball against his chest. The ball feels vaguely damp. The ball smells bad. He drops it in the hamper and he shuts the lid. Old man, he thinks. You smelly, dirty, sad old sack of man.

He tugs the hamper, but it feels too heavy to be lifted. He stoops down and drags the hamper from the bed frame to the door. It leaves a line of long, deep grooves inside the freshly vacuumed carpet.

When the hamper butts against the door, he clasps his hands against his knees, exhales dry, charred sounds, like burning leaves. He cracks the door. He peers into the empty, quiet hall. He can just barely hear the clink of distant silver, tables being set.

He slides the hamper out into the hall, before the door.

He squints. He hears a woman's laughter rising through the silver sound.

It is a warm laugh. A familiar laugh. A laugh he knows but cannot put a name to.

•

A knock. A woman's voice. Good morning, dear.

Good morning, he calls back. He smiles as the voice opens the door.

It's Ms. Tanya. He knows her name because she wears a name tag. A pink uniform. She has a gap between her teeth.

She smiles. Sit down, dear, she says.

He sits. She straps the cuff around his thin white skin. She pumps the tube. It hisses. She writes down some numbers on the chart.

He coughs. What's that? The day I'm gonna die?

She laughs. You're funny, honey.

Yeah, he says. But looks aren't everything.

You're looking good, she says. She edges up the velcro of the cuff. She tears it very slowly so she doesn't hurt him.

His skin pricks, not from pain, but from the effort. Sad old man, he thinks. He glances at the gap between her teeth.

Thank you, Ms. Tanya, he says.

My pleasure. Her tooth gap whistles. She walks toward the window, and she stands there.

Her silhouette against the curtain makes him think about his wife. It's something in the way she holds her shoulders.

He watches as she shrugs, stretches her back, pinches a strand of hair, and sighs, pushing it back behind her ear.

It's such a pretty day, she says. Light breeze. Low 70s.

He smiles. Good. I hope that you get to enjoy it.

•

After Ms. Tanya helps him choose his clothes—tan pants, a rust-brown checkered shirt that feels like the fabric of an old couch—he stands, slouches in his walker, pushes himself down the hall. He listens as the gentle, clinking silver sound grows closer, louder.

He sees another woman in pink uniform pushing another resident who sits, sunk down, into his wheelchair.

The resident is wrapped inside a blue fleece blanket.

Like a baby, he thinks, relieved he is still—at least—a man.

•

His walker rounds the curve into the dining room. The silver sound builds from a tinny echo to a symphony of scraping knives. A table full of men with plates—all wearing checkered shirts—looks up across the room and nods and waves for him to join them.

Top of the mornin' to you, says one.

Light breeze. 70s, another says.

They give his back a friendly pat as he sits in his chair.

Sleep well? They ask.

He clears his throat, which means both yes and no.

Not me, says one of them. Terrible dreams again. The war.

They all nod.

A young girl carries his tray to the table. He looks at the tendril curls of hair escaping from her net. He thinks, that's nice. She sets his tray in front of him. A tattoo, on her wrist. A skull with roses. He thinks, well, now, that is not so nice.

Breakfast appears to be three pale palm-sized pancakes, two small links of shiny sausage, a sulfuric-smelling yellow scoop of scramble, and the ever-present teacup filled with coffee, which he reaches for, dismayed by the slight tremble of his hands.

The table of his friends sits, sipping, silent, mostly.

Coughing.

Sipping.

Someone reads the paper, turns the page.

Somebody clears his throat. Good news in there?

Nope, says the paper-holder. War, there. Everywhere. Out there, he sighs.

They all nod, knowingly.

•

Out there, a small brown finch is hopping on the lawn. He watches from the window as the brown finch flits along a patch of high grass.

The finch jumps, catches at the grass, and grabs a bit of grain. A long strand bounces back and forth. The bird keeps jumping, catching, grabbing.

Then, another finch flies down to join the first.

They jump.

They catch.

They nibble at the air.

Another bird flies down.

Another.

And another.

Soon, the lawn is filled with hopping, jumping finches, strands of light grass gently quivering amid their movements.

•

A memory begins to quiver in his brain.

Something about the window.

Watching something through the window, at home, with his wife.

He can remember her back, silhouetted, shadowed.

Coming up behind her.

Circling his arms around her waist.

Leaning to kiss her cheek.

Her tendril curls of hair.

Catching a strand between his fingertips.

Pushing the strand behind her ear.

The smell of her perfume.
The way she smelled…like what?
Lilac?
Or violet?
His thoughts contract.
The moment stirs.
Its thin strands split.
It slips away.

•

The silver scrapes, then stutters to a stop. The old men yawn. The small brown finches fly away. The tattooed girl comes by to take their trays. The rose skull circles round the table, darting in and out until it hovers—white-gray, flecked with red—in front of him.

    He frowns. What made you want to get that tattoo, there? He says.
    She sighs. I was so young, then.
    He says, you are still so young.
    He laughs.
    She laughs.
    He says, someday, you'll be a good wife to someone.
    She says, haha.
    She does not laugh.
    He says, you should remove it.
    She says, sure.

•

The women in pink uniforms drift through the room and down the hall. The building softens to the long hush of the afternoon. Every now and then, a short alarm goes off. The pink suits scatter. Mostly, though, the men sit, silent, shuffling their cards.

    They mumble, scratch.
    Mhm. Mhm.
    They flip their cards onto the table.

Rummy! One declares.

God damn it, no. We're playing Hearts.

They whisper, shuffle.

In the far back corner of the room, a fish tank bubbles. Flashes of fins dart through the tank's dim, violet glow.

He thinks, violet.

Lilac.

Gin!

God damn it, no.

He thinks of pink light.

Thinks of shadows, thinks he was once married. Once. He must have been.

•

The sun's light swells into the shade he's thinking of, which makes the room feel like a scene he's conjured from a dream. He hears an eerie resonance amid the low hum of the fish tank, thinks the whispered, shuffled cards sound like the wisps of wings.

An old woman enters the room. She passes by the table carrying a pad of a paper and a box of paint. She wears her white-gray hair pinned in a thick curl with an indentation at its center, like a little nest. She wears a filmy scarf, a button blouse, a long skirt filled with flowers in the same pastel shades as his pale pastel sheets.

He sniffs, picks up a strain of her perfume. That smell. Those flowers.

He looks up above the hands, the murmured sounds, his fan of cards.

He watches her sit down, spread out her paper and her paint.

He plays a diamond, takes the round. He sweeps the cards into his stack.

She dips her brush into a glass of water, picks a color. Dips her brush into the glass. The water streams with blue.

Somebody says, the thing about the war…not just our town…the country…an entire country…an entire generation lost.

Somebody says, the field…
Someone else says, in the forest…mud…the rain…
He wonders if they're thinking of the same war.
He looks up again.
The water's stained with deep blue, violet, gray.
She stirs. The water turns a shade of milky lilac blue.
The war…the thing about the war…
Hell, someone murmurs. War is hell.
He thinks, that color is the color of the scent he cannot name.
He pardons himself from the table when the game is finished, starts to makes his way toward the woman's corner of the room.
Going to see about a lady? Ask the men.
He chuckles drily in response.

•

She looks up, startled, as his walker butts into the table's edge.
Seat taken? He asks.
She says, I suppose not.
He sits down. Nice day, he says. Light breeze. 70s.
Yes, so they say, she says. She looks back down and contemplates her painting.
He watches for awhile as she nods above her painting, pushes back the tails of her scarf, which drift down, once again. He watches her expression, twitching corners of her mouth. The empty indentation of her coiled nest of hair.
Your perfume. What's that scent? He asks.
She dabs. It's lavender, she says.
Ah, lavender, he says. I like it very much.
I used to grow it in my garden, when I had a garden. She smiles lightly, stirs the water, which then turns a deep, bright blue.
He tries to picture his backyard, which had a garden. He does not remember what was growing in it. He spent mornings on the front lawn, trimming long, green grooves that spiraled from the yard's periphery into its fresh mown heart.

He says, a garden is a good thing. Good place for a woman.

I do miss the garden, she says. All the birds and butterflies. But that was long ago. She makes an odd sound, like she's sipping from the air. For one breath of a moment, she sounds like a little girl.

She looks at him. He looks at her. There's something so familiar, yet so unfamiliar in her face. Her skin is full of lines, so many pathways to get lost in. He tries to look through them, searching for something he recognizes.

Do I know you? She says, suddenly.

He sips the air. He sounds old.

He says, possibly. I think, maybe, you do.

They lock eyes, once again. Her smile broadens.

She says, maybe. Lightly, as though brushing at the edges of some secret they might share.

They sit there, looking at each other, for another moment.

Then, Ms. Tanya comes up to the table, nods down at the painting.

Is it finished, dear?

I think so.

Let me take the glass.

Ms. Tanya carries off her little tumbler of bright blue.

•

That evening, he stands, looking at himself inside the mirror. He thinks, smelly, dirty, sad old sack of man. He makes himself laugh at this thought. He laughs at himself laughing. Then, he watches how his face goes slack when he removes the teeth.

He pours a spot of Listerine into his glass.

The same bright blue.

His teeth sit, like a fossil in some fish-less sea.

He looks intently at the glass, the shade of blue. His mind strains at his eyes. He feels his veins begin to ache.

He shuffles back into the bedroom. Gray-blue light seeps through the curtains and some frail sense of recognition starts to filter through.

A knock, then, interrupts his thoughts. It is Ms. Tanya. She brings in his laundry hamper filled with clean, warm, floral-scented sheets.

He thinks they look like something that a woman would pick out. He can't remember purchasing or picking out these sheets.

She helps him make the bed. She tugs and smoothes its surface. Then, she stretches by the window, yawns, and tucks her hair back into place.

The gray-blue light surrounds her, silhouettes her frame.

Is everything okay with you, tonight? Ms. Tanya asks.

He says, I don't think so. I cannot find my wife.

Ms. Tanya smiles, but her smile has an odd look to it.

She leans down and she opens his top drawer.

She lays his bed clothes out over the sheets.

Laid out this way, his thinks that they look like a shapeless man.

Let's get some rest, she says. I'll help you find your wife tomorrow.

•

He squints into the morning light. He slips his feet into his slippers, ties his robe. He pads into the bathroom, to the toilet.

This morning is a stronger, strangely pinkish stream of piss.

He thinks about the light.

About his wife.

He flushes.

•

A knock. Ms. Tanya enters, carrying a package.

Today is your birthday, she says. Happy Birthday, dear.

How old am I, today? He asks.

She says, older than me.

He chuckles. Pretty old then, huh?

Her tooth gap whistles.

Ms. Tanya opens and unpacks the box. She hands him every item as she takes it out. The box contains a pack of undershirts, a new hand towel, and a small rectangle box of brand name chocolates.

He holds the objects in his hands. He turns them over, looks at them. They all have no significance to him.

Can't eat those with my teeth, he gestures at the chocolates.

It's the thought that counts, I guess, she shrugs apologetically.

•

He sits down with the table of his men. A pink suit carries him a tray with coffee, brown toast, thin grits, and a dish of fruit cocktail with tiny specks of pink, but mostly filled with whole, white, peeled, vulnerable grapes.

Top of the mornin' to you, says one.

High of 67. Chance of showers in the afternoon, another says.

He pictures showers in the afternoon. Small drops of memory begin to trickle through the gray-blue of his mind.

Today's my birthday, he announces.

Happy Birthday, they congratulate him. Why, you old son of a gun.

They all nod, knowingly. They look back down into their breakfast.

The grits taste like quicksand. The toast, like ordinary sand.

One of the men begins to cough. They all ignore it, for a moment, but the cough grows louder and much more insistent. A pink suit flutters from across the room. She pats the man's back firmly til he gags a wet pink fleck of cherry.

The man looks down until she leaves. He shakes his head. I don't know what came over me, just now, he says. I'm so embarrassed.

One of them nods with understanding. One time, I was so embarrassed.

The men lean in to hear him tell the story.

We all were riding on the bus, you know, he says, somewhere in Italy. The hills were steep, you know. The bus was curling, right along the edge. The hills were high, not much to keep us almost from the edge. So, anyhow. The driver, I don't think he knew what he was doing. So, he gets pulled over, so, he stops, and then the door just opens. All these men, the police—we were all in Italy—they had these great big guns, you know, these just enormous guns over their shoulders, and well, there we were. They had these great big guns, in Italy.

    Today's your birthday, huh. The men look back toward him.

    I suppose so.

    They all sing together: Happy Birthday, Happy Birthday to you.

    One of their voices cracks in his attempt to sing the harmony.

    They all look down as though they were the culprit.

•

The sky darkens from gray-blue into deeper gray. The rain begins to fall. It falls hard, fogging up the windows. Through the windows, he can see the soft, blurred shapes of trees, the softly glowing globe lamps, haloed all around the building.

    An old woman with white-gray hair pinned in a thick curl walks into the room, holding a pad of a paper and a pack of paint. She glances toward him as she passes by the table, and the men grin. Looks like you had better follow her.

    He sits across from her as she sets up her paper and her paint.

    He breathes in.

    Lilac.

    Violet.

    No, lavender.

    Your lavender perfume, he nods.

    She nods. That's right. My garden, when I had one.

    Yes, your garden. He remembers, now. For now.

    She dabs her paintbrush, dips into the glass. A spot of tea-green sheds its pale strands. She stirs. The strands dissolve.

    The wind begins to blow the rain in sheets, which hit the glass, then splatter streams of gray-blue-gleaming water.

    The spring is bittersweet, she says. The rain.

    Don't much get out no more, in rain nor shine, he chuckles airily.

    I mean the way the rain reminds me of my garden, looking at it from the window, waiting to get out, she says.

She dabs her brush. She dips. The water streams with reddish-brown, the shade of things in disrepair, the shade of rusting tools. Then, she stirs. The water turns a murky puddle-brown. He thinks of oil, thinks of sawdust, thinks of afternoons in his garage.

When I look out the window in the rain, she says, sometimes I think the garden will be there, just waiting, when the rain clears.

He says, that's a nice thought. A garden is a good thing. Good place for a woman.

While it lasts, she sighs. She stirs the paint.

Somewhere off down the hall, somebody fingers at an old piano. A few hesitant keys, then a set of scales. First, descending. Then, ascending, with an air of distant optimism. The piano lingers, echoing above the highest note.

It plays some breezy melody, all brightly flitting pecks of keys and warm chords.

She sighs, shakes her head, and dabs her brush. She paints. She stirs.

The song ends. A small group of unseen hands claps, slightly.

A new song begins. He trains his ears. This one, he thinks that he might know.

He strains his thoughts toward the movements of the keys, into anticipation of the verse.

He starts to sing. The voice that comes out of his mouth is strangely frail. He has never heard this voice before:

*Today, while the blossoms still cling to the vine.*
*I'll taste your sweet berries, I'll drink your sweet wine.*
*A million tomorrows will all pass away.*
*Ere I forget all the joy that is mine.*
*Today.*

They laugh together, at his voice, and at the song.

Your voice is lovely, she exclaims.

Come now, he coughs.

It is though. Lovely.

He looks at her eyes and at their gentle shining folds, a bit like petals from a wilted rose.

They linger, speechless, in the kind of cloudy feeling that piano adaptations of familiar music always brings. His ears continue scanning melodies for bits he knows. He watches her keep dabbing, stirring, dabbing, stirring, smearing paint.

The water in the glass does not evoke the sense of recognition that it did, though, when it turned bright blue before. It just turns brown, then brown, then darker-brown, then dark-brown, then dark-dark-brown, then dark-darker-brown, then gray-dark-brown, then black.

What are you painting, there? He asks.

She turns the picture upright, so the bits of wet paint drizzle weakly down the page.

I'm trying, she says, but I can't…

The teary stems, the bright, smudged orbs, look like the painting of a child, nothing like a garden.

Then, the piano starts to play a flat, chordless rendition of the Happy Birthday song. Strange distant voices chorus, Happy Birthday, Happy Birthday, and Ms. Tanya scurries in, holding a cupcake with a candle.

Happy Birthday! Says Ms. Tanya.

Happy Birthday! Says the older woman.

Happy Birthday! Sing the voices of the strangers he can't see.

He leans in, takes a deep breath, and blows out the candle.

Distant hands clap for him.

Smoke drifts over everything.

•

He dreams in flickers. Flashes. Gray-blue. Coffee. Shadows. Lace. A smile. Hair tucked back. A silhouette. Blue flowers in a blue vase. Thin bones. Thin, thin, brittle. False teeth. Outlines in the bed. A dream about an old dream. Cold fog. Dreams about the war, the war, the war. Always the war. Cold fog. Brown puddles. Yellow gas. Blue flowers. Yellow-brown. Thin bones, exposed. The weight of them. The dreamlike movements. Cold fog. Thin, thin, brittle, never able to move fast enough. Gray-blue. The sense that something—waiting to consume you—lives beneath the air.

•

He peers into the light. A haze of white-gray, shivering with dust. He aches. He slips feet into slippers, shoulders into robe.

    His chest hurts and he coughs.
    He has to still himself against the door frame.
    He tears up, involuntarily.
    He pisses puddle brown.

•

He waits for her amid the shuffled whispers of the cards.
    The murmured expletives: God damn it, no. Sonofabitch.
    The muffled coughs.
    Bad rain all week, and thunderstorms. Low 60s.
    Coffee tastes like mud.
    The war, the war.
    The thing about the war…

•

He waits for her amid the movements of the light, the weather, hoping her shape will materialize with the slightest change.
    But she does not materialize.
    Nothing ever changes.
    He just moves throughout the day, as usual, perceiving flickers in the air.

•

He dreams in flickers. Pink light. Gray-blue drifts. Flakes of dust. Flakes of ashes, falling. Sawdust. Shavings. Smell of sulfur. Smell of paint. Smell of the coffee, brewing through the day. The smell of an eternal morning. Shadows moving. Nothing ever changes.

Until: one morning, he wakes up, and he can smell his own breath.
   It is terrible.
   The fibers of his robe feel like fine needles, sewn together.
   When he stands, he nearly falls.
   When he leans down to piss, he nearly falls.
   A bad piss.
   Red.
   He shivers deeply in his bones.

•

He dreams long lace shadows like the lattice of his veins. Hair blowing. Silhouettes he follows, but he cannot reach. Cold. Thin bones. Empty bed. Cold fog. The war the war the war the war the war the word, the word war, wife, the word wife, wife, the missing wife.
   The flickers turn to flames which turn to nightmares. Gray-blue caverns that he wanders through, into a black-blue maw. He falls. He falls into a forest, which he realizes is a graveyard, which he realizes is a clay trench, filled with fallen forms.
   He wakes and stares into the curtains, terrified to fall asleep. He lies, looking up at the ceiling, at the circle of the light, which looks back, humming, lidless, like a peeled eye. He sweats and sweats and sweats and shivers, staring as hard as he can.

•

Ms. Tanya comes into his room holding a cup of tea.
   Good morning, dear.
   What's good about it? He says.
   Yeah, well, she agrees.
   She sets the cup of tea beside his bed. She sits beside his bed, carefully folds the strip around his arm, and gently pumps.
   It feels like the air is being sucked out of his skin. He makes a

hissing sound, like sipping from the air. The sound reminds him of his wife. My wife. What happened to my wife? He asks Ms. Tanya.

She looks out the window.

I'm sorry, but she's gone, she says, after a moment.

Gone?

She nods.

Do you know where? He says.

She says, no. I am sorry.

He says, don't be, and looks where she is looking through the window. He sees a sliver of a tree. An empty parking lot.

He looks into his tea. He stirs the trails from the leaves.

They flow like fingers through the water, in a sort of warm wave.

He holds the cup between his hands.

He breathes in, sips.

He stirs.

He smiles, his hands tingling.

Hello.

# SKIN

Your eyes are closed.
    Your hand is open in my hand.
    Your mouth opens. It closes.
    Opens. Closes. Opens. Closes.
    It opens all the way, then only halfway.
    Then, it hovers there.
    A silence, for a moment, then a sound.

•

I think of stove pots boiling, sounds of liquid in distress.
    The gentle, necessary flicking of a switch.
    I think of you, there, sipping tea.
    Or you, there, spooning soup.
    Or you, there, stirring something.
    Doing something.
    Being there.

•

Some time goes by, and I go out to get some air.
    I stand out in the yard, before your window, looking at a tree.
    The wind stirs intermittently.
    The tree stands, shivering.
    Its frail skin flutters, like feathers of bodiless birds.

# TO HOLD, TO HOLLOW

The sensation of sleep. The sensation of unknown sensation that hums in your hollows. The sensation of waking, forgetting, remembering, fading, and failing, dissembling. The sensation of waking up early, head hard, eyes like cold bullets under your lids. The sensation of squinting, thin needles of light, as your hand guides your mind through the room. The sensation of rising and yawning and swallowing sour taste, spitting it out. The sensation of sitting in front of your mother's lap, letting her brush all the snarls from your hair. The sensation of tugging, of ripping, of hissing, hold still, in your ear. The sensation of wriggling, whining, of gritting your teeth, as you try to count backward from ten. The sensation of standing up with her beside you, and looking inside of the mirror, as she tousles and twists up your hair, clipping, hold still. The sensation that you are bad. The sensation of sewing, of training your eyes through the needle, through one, thin, minuscule slit, pinching tight to the edge of your thread, licking lightly, the tip. The sensation of pulling it through. The sensation of watching your grandmother sewing, hands feeding the fabric along the machine with its jagged tooth, gnawing its pathway of perfectly hashed lines. The sensation of running out into the snow. The sensation of ruining shoes. The sensation of tracking in mud, in the dark, unaware, switching on the light, feeling the fear in your throat. The sensation of spilling root beer on your pristine new white Easter sweater. The sensation of dropping a plate and the instant of hoping before the plate shatters. The sensation of picking up fragments, of piercing your skin, the air rushing inside of the opening, filling you with a sharp chill. The sensation that you are bad. The sensation of petting the cat. The sensation of getting a scratch. The sensation of swimming in cold water, toweling off, drying off, diving back in. The sensation of riding around in the back seat and listening to your CDs, watching mountains unfurl, hills wane, cities sprawl, and tall trees shed their leaves. The sensation of looking out windows, of looking at pictures in albums, of looking at sculptures of Jesus, of looking at magazines, looking at art. The sensation of looking at girls. The sensation of noticing something you like, or would like to have, like to have been, or be, someday, you hope to become. The sensation of touching your tongue to a sore in your mouth, licking secretive wounds. The sensation of something all wrong in your underwear, cotton that catches inside of your crotch. The sensation of cutting your hair. The sensation of dying your hair blue, then black. The sensation of switching to new underwear, smoother fabric that lets you forget what it hides. The sensation of stepping up onto the scale, the fluttering sound as it settles in place. The sensation of pinching your waist in an effort to see how much of yourself you can still hold. The sensation of tossing some twigs of spaghetti into a hot pot, and then watching them boil. The sensation of watching the dish in the microwave, turning and turning. The sensation of peeling an orange. The sensation of pouring some flakes. The sensation of waiting for coffee, then sipping the first hot sip, tenderly, carefully. The sensation of scratching an itch. The sensation of thick, itchy sweaters. The sensation of twirling, of pinning up your hair, the twisting of your wrist. The sensation of opening up the front door. The sensation of stepping out onto the ice. The sensation of stepping out into the sun. The sensation of stepping out into the rain. The sensation of racing to catch the bus, catching your breath in its smog. The sensation of catching a woman's reflection inside of the window, inside of your own. The sensation of quickening pulse. The sensation of jittering floors. The sensation of cold. The sensation of watching her face as she looks at you, knowing that you have been looking too long. The sensation of seeing her shift to avoid you. The sensation that you are bad. The sensation of picking your chapped lips and biting inside of your cheek. The sensation of pressing your face to the window and watching the street fogging by. The sensation of clasping your hands around warm coffee, cooler now, safer to sip. The sensation of walking up long flights of stairs. The sensation of sitting beneath a bright light. The sensation of humming vibrations sent down from the light, and absorbed by your skin. The sensation of stretching, and pacing, and trips to the semi public bathroom. The sensation of scanning the bottoms of stalls to see if there are feet underneath them. The sensation of waiting, foot tapping, and catching a thin whiff of piss. The sensation of ducking in, squatting, and training your ears as you piss, shit, covertly. The sensation of pulling your underwear back up, still loose, still the same, smooth synthetic. The sensation of pumping a foamy white soap mound and rinsing it off. The sensation of sitting down back at your desk. The sensation of coffee, gone cold. The sensation of typing, and pausing, and typing, and straining, and pausing to stretch out your hands, and you do so by clasping, unclasping your fist, and you do so by clenching, unclenching your fingers, and opening them, and then closing them, stretching them out toward the light. The sensation of hoping for something to hold. The sensation of holding a drink. The sensation of drinking a bourbon Manhattan and sucking the cherry. The sensation of stirring your cocktail sword. The sensation of picking your teeth with it. The sensation of tingling sharpness that digs in the grooves of your gums. The sensation of digging around in your purse for the compact mirror, fixing your lipstick. The sensation of checking your teeth, which somehow always seem to get covered in red. The sensation of waiting, and waiting. The sensation when she arrives, or he arrives. The sensation of looking him over, her over, brown hair, black hair, gray hair, and touching your own. The sensation of standing and sliding across from, beside her, or him. The sensation of speaking, adjusting your voice. The sensation of bass seeping, glass clinking, TV commercials, all muffled together, a too thick scarf of sounds around your words. The sensation of swallowing, gulping, of looking up, down, and around, to hear what they are saying. The sensation of a hand placed on your hand, the permission to leave. The sensation of walking up long flights of stairs. The sensation of walking into a dark room, where the light flicks behind you, illuminating a strange space. The sensation of having another drink, which you know that you won't finish, then leaning in, letting them lean in, or kneel, or kneeling to kiss them, or letting them kiss you. The sensation of smell. The sensation of taste. The sensation of most of it, strong, dark, and sour, or mint flavored, recently mint flavored, starting to fade. The sensation of a couch, a bed, a hard, soft, wall, so many textures, sounds, arrangements of their unfamiliarity. The sensation of standing, of straddling, fingering, sucking, secreting, of touching things, taking things, making things do things, and thus, making things into things. The sensation of an arm, a leg, a knee, an elbow, wrapping, or unwrapping, bumping up against your arm, your leg, your knee. The sensation of a new smell, salivation mixed with bergamot, synthetic pine sprig into sweat, tea rose into genital juice. The sensation of a cunt, a cock, a tongue, a who knows what, a something wet, a kiss, a flip, a lick, a lip, a sniff, a shift, a slide, a cough, a creak, a web of wet hair in your face, a pimple, nipple, pink, or brown, amid a tuft, a mound, a round, a soft, flat mass, amid a body, short, or long, or smooth, or furred, or sharp, or stiff, or swimming up to you, then backward as you move your mouth, your hands, your face, your mouth, your hands, your face, your face, your face, a face you cannot see, you never see, you never do see what you want to when you think, feeling around, the moment when you make it come, the cunt, her cunt, the cock, his cock, the face, their face, your face, your face, your face, your face. The sensation that you are bad. The sensation of the underwear, picked up and put back on. The sensation of a brush torn through the snarls of your hair. The sensation of your quiet footsteps through the strange room, to the door. The sensation of opening, ducking your head in the wind. The sensation of huddling into your coat. The sensation of walking out into the dark. The sensation of an echoed engine, quivering the streets, the way small cities hollow themselves out late in the night. The sensation of an oil smell, a gravel smell. The sensation of walking by a vent from which a thick, grey steam is pouring. The sensation of climbing back up to your room, into your bed, and wrapping yourself deep inside the shadows of your sheets. The sensation of waking up, sick. The sensation of coughing and holding your chest. The sensation of smelling like sweat, mostly yours, some of theirs, mixed with bergamot. The sensation of lying, and coughing, and reaching your arm out, and pouring a cap full of syrup, a cup full of bourbon, and swallowing, switching them back and forth, and back and forth. The sensation of watching TV. The sensation of ordering lunch. The sensation of hot noodles, slimy green peppers, and bean curd. The sensation of cold and half-hardened white rice. The sensation of opening packets of sauce with your teeth. The sensation of drizzling them over everything. The sensation of swallowing, painfully, chewing each bite twenty times, in the way you were taught. The sensation of warm spit, full stomach, disgust. The sensation that you are bad. The sensation of chopping up garlic and ginger, then smelling the tips of your fingers, then thinking of other times when you have made this same motion, have done this same act, with quite different results. The sensation of tossing some vegetables into a pan full of oil, and frying them up. The sensation of eating too quickly and burning your mouth. The sensation of running your injured tongue over your teeth as you package the leftovers, shelve them inside of the fridge, and then stand for a minute, inside of the droning blue glow. The sensation of taking a bath, lying back in the water, and letting it flow through your hair, fill your ears and your nose and all your other openings. The sensation of shaving your legs. The sensation of nicking your skin with the blade. The sensation of raising your ankle, blood running, and dabbing it off with a rag. The sensation of tracing a clear circle into the mirror fog, feathering out your hair, wondering what you would look like with shorter bangs, longer hair, shorter hair, flipped to the side. The sensation of Googling girls with good hair. The sensation of Googling girls with short hair. The sensation of Googling girls with short lavender hair. The sensation of Googling girls with short lavender hair, puffy nipples, and small breasts, unfurling your skirt with one hand, scrolling search images with the other. The sensation of wishing your breasts looked like that. The sensation of touching them, feeling dissatisfied with the sensation of something so yours and so known. The sensation of searching for lavender lingerie, pale gray stockings with lavender seams. The sensation of buying a set of sheer panties in orchid and aubergine, on sale. The sensation of buying a gimlet, to try it, a dirty martini, a dry one, then back to the dirty one, briny as yes, you know what, because who are you kidding. The sensation of meeting a lawyer who says he likes secrets. The sensation of meeting a stripper who says she likes dogs. The sensation of meeting an art teacher with a blonde streak in her blunt cut black hair, who declares she is looking for someone to keep her company. The sensation of meeting a surgeon who carries a very large purse filled with boxes of dark purple nitrile gloves that she puts on whenever she smokes. The sensation of fucking inside of the book store, the library, bathroom, the back room, inside of the back of the booth, on the twenty-fourth floor of the merchandise mart. The sensation of sex on the table, the counter, the window, the balcony, in an abandoned warehouse, on a brittle concrete slab outside a train yard. The sensation of making a list of things that you would like to do, doing them, ticking them off. The sensation of reading it, trying to read something into it, failing. The sensation of reading a book without reading it, paging through, thinking, I'm in here, somewhere. The sensation of touching yourself in your bed without touching much, thinking, I'm in here, somewhere. The sensation holding your skirt as the wind blows too strong. The sensation of holding the edge of your flimsy umbrella against a hard rain. The sensation of stepping around puddles, seepages, islands of muddy wet trash. The sensation of riding the bus, nodding off on the window, with bags at your feet. The sensation of ending up at the wrong stop. The sensation of wandering, squinting around. The sensation of seeing a house that looks just like your grandmother's. The sensation of memory, pale teal tile, pile carpet, a big picture window, and shelves full of thick picture albums and magazines, statues of Jesus. The sensation of memory, hide and seek, ducking in showers, in closets, behind the dark doors of the wardrobe, beneath the mothball scented sweaters and coats. The sensation of memory, pastel smocks, hair curlers, tufts of white hair wisping out of them, smiling, tea stained teeth with gold plated caps on the side of a mouth, gleaming strangely. The sensation of cold feet, cold nipples, cold lit, distant windows, like teeth. The sensation of betrayal when an unknown man walks by, inside. The sensation of going inside. The sensation of closing the door, turning off all the lights. The sensation of licking an envelope, sealing it shut. The sensation of sermons, of funerals, dim lit wood paneling, weak coffee brewing. The sensation of weddings and showers and new dresses bought to wear to them. The sensation of curling your hair overnight, and unrolling the rollers, next morning, to find that the right side is perfect, the left, a complete utter mess. The sensation of taking a brush to the right side and making it wrong, so it matches the left, tearing hard, frizzing up all the edges, and tossing your head in a frenzy. The sensation of biting your nails. The sensation of punching the wall. The sensation of fingering, fisting, of slapping, and biting, and digging around in someone else's shape. The sensation of coming, hard, feeling your muscles protracting and pushing themselves from your bones. The sensation of coming, soft, looking up into the globe lamp, cocooning its light. The sensation of snow falling, coating the world in its sheen. The sensation of melting, uncoating, revealing, of having learned nothing from years worth of seasons. The sensation of plays and recitals and concerts and trivia nights and bar hopping and team meetings, bowling and badminton, brunches and birthdays and date nights and calling in sick. The sensation of Fridays, and Saturdays, Sundays, and Mondays, and Tuesdays, and Wednesdays, and Thursdays, and Fridays, and more dates and drinks, and more sleeping, and eating, and meeting, and kissing, and fucking, and shaving, and cutting your hair short, and growing it out, and more chasing the bus, and more looking through windows, at windows, and watching them, waiting for something, some portal, some image, some message, to play there, forever, of riding the bus and imagining mountains unfurling, hills waning, in place of the parking lots, blocks with the same signs recurring, the same scenes repeated, of hunger, of fullness, of happiness, boredom, and waiting, and waiting, and anxiousness, which is just really a form of some sourceless, eternal impatience, of here and of gone, and of now, and of dull, and of fear, and of done, and of shame, and of farce, and of love, and of guilt, and of vague pain, vague hope, and vague longing, vague sadness, vague pleasure, vague loss. The sensation of loss. The sensation of loss. The sensation of loss.

Special thanks to the following people, without whom this book would not exist: Jason Pappariella, James Tadd Adcox, M. Kitchell, Robert Kloss, Christine Schutt, Lynne Tillman, Kathryn Davis, Danielle Dutton, Marshall Klimasewiski, my Washington University colleagues, and (of course) Richard Siken and Drew Burk. Extra special thanks to Lucy, Gregory, Artemis, and Icarus (my non-human muses).

**MEGHAN LAMB** is from Illinois and has lived (variously) throughout Indiana, Ohio, Washington, Pennsylvania, Connecticut, and Eastern Europe.

CPSIA information can be obtained
at www.ICGtesting.com
Printed in the USA
BVHW031657130320
574905BV00002B/8